CHANCE IS ABOUT TO TAKE THE PLUNGE

"So you kill me to eliminate your problem," Chance said, stalling for time. If he could keep this weasel talking, he might—just might—find a way to extricate himself. After all, all he had to do was overcome four human gorillas and somehow manage to evade the Colt that Calloway kept leveled at his chest. The odds weren't the greatest, but they were all he had.

"I've no intention of killing you, Sharpe," Calloway said. "I'll let the river take care of you."

Without so much as a grunt, the two overmuscled apes in human clothing stepped forward with island-sized paws outstretched to snare their helpless prey...

CHANCE

#12

WHITE WATER

CLAY TANNER

AVON BOOKS ◆ NEW YORK

CHANCE #12: WHITE WATER is an original publication of Avon Books. This work has never before appeared in book form.

AVON BOOKS
A division of
The Hearst Corporation
105 Madison Avenue
New York, New York 10016

Copyright © 1988 by George W. Proctor
Published by arrangement with the author
Library of Congress Catalog Card Number: 87-91840
ISBN: 0-380-75524-6

First Avon Books Printing: July 1988

AVON TRADEMARK REG. U.S. PAT. OFF. AND IN OTHER COUNTRIES, MARCA REGISTRADA, HECHO EN U.S.A.

Printed in the U.S.A.

K–R   10   9   8   7   6   5   4   3   2   1

To my grandfather, Hap Ferris,
the rumors of whose death
have not been exaggerated,
as a thank-you for my introduction
to Mark Twain

ONE

A bluff is a bluff. No matter how a man cocks his head from side to side or squints his eyes doesn't alter the situation. A bluff remains a bluff.

Which was exactly what Chance Sharpe held. The riverboat gambler's steel blue eyes dipped to the five blue-backed cards fanned in his hand. A pair of deuces wasn't the foundation for a firm wager—especially when five hundred dollars lay on the table.

"I'll take two," a cotton merchant seated across the green felt-covered table said, drawing two of the cards from his hand and tossing them down. A shadow of disappointment darkened the man's eyes when he lifted the pair of cards the dealer placed before him.

No improvement, Chance thought. He had read the merchant like a book throughout the evening. At best the man held a pair, had asked for two cards to hide his weak hand, hoping to draw a triplet, and had failed. When the betting began anew, the merchant would fold.

The two cards that Riley Tombaugh requested brought no telltale flicker to the man's brown eyes. Tombaugh, a Louisiana rice-grower, was a cool one. The money he placed on the table would be the only clue to the cards he held. The man was too conservative a poker player to bet on anything that wasn't a winning hand.

The two men to Tombaugh's left both asked for two cards and winced when they glanced at the cards dealt them. The gambler needed to know nothing else about their hands.

1

"One," Brad Calloway said with a nod to the dealer.

Chance knew nothing about Calloway, except his name and that he had boarded the *Gulf Runner* shortly before the sternwheeler pulled out from St. Louis that morning. The gambler was cognizant of that last fact simply because Calloway had crossed the gangway onto the *Gulf Runner*'s main deck two strides ahead of Chance.

As to what the man's hand contained, Chance could only guess. While Calloway had won a couple of hands early in the evening, he had been a heavy loser ever since. Twice he had gone to the wallet inside his coat to renew the money he kept on the table.

"I'll take two." The dealer took his own draw, then glanced at the gambler.

The trouble with a bluff is that for it to work a man must play it and not worry about the consequences. After a night of steady winning hands, Chance had proven to the players with him at the table that he was a man who backed up his bets with power. If there were a time perfectly suited to a bluff, it was now.

"I'll stand pat." Chance took a long, slender, black saber cigar from his coat and lit it. Through the smoke of his first puff, he saw Tombaugh's and Calloway's gazes shoot to him. The gambler smiled inwardly; he had given both men something to mull over.

"And you, Mr. Winslow?" the dealer asked the last man at the table, who took two cards and bit his lower lip. "I believe the bet's with Mr. Winslow."

"Five dollars." The man beside Chance edged five silver dollars into the pot as though he parted with a fortune.

"Your five and twenty-five of my own." This from the cotton merchant, to Chance's surprise.

"An additional fifty," Tombaugh said without hesitation, shoving four twenty-dollar gold pieces to the center of the table.

The two players to the rice-grower's left blanched and folded. Calloway reached into his wallet and withdrew a single bill that he tossed atop the pot with an arrogant flick of the wrist. "Make it an even hundred."

The dealer shook his head as he dropped his cards to the table. "Too rich for my blood."

For a pair-of-deuces bluff to work, a man had to drive off the other players with the only strength left to him— cold, hard cash. Chance met the hundred and upped the pot another hundred dollars.

Winslow and the cotton merchant closed their fanned hands and plopped them to the table with shakes of their heads. Tombaugh studied his hand a moment then glanced at the money stacked on the table before him. "I'm a hundred twenty shy. Another thirty will make it a hundred fifty."

The rice-grower counted out one hundred fifty dollars, then abruptly placed another fifty atop the pile of bills, making his bump eighty.

A barely discernible tremble quivered through Calloway's fingers as he slipped them into his coat to withdraw the wallet once again. Pulling a single hundred-dollar bill out, he dropped it atop the pot. Small beads of sweat glistened across the man's brow as he shoved the wallet back into his coat pocket.

Empty wallet, Chance thought as he lifted three hundred from the money stacked on the table before him. "I'll see the hundred to me and raise two hundred." Unless he misjudged, Calloway was tapped out, leaving Tombaugh for the showdown.

For a long silent moment the rice-grower stared at the five cards while the fingers of his left hand tapped his own stack of bills. Tombaugh drew a heavy breath and exhaled it in a gust of disgust. "Should have had the sense to throw these cards away when they were dealt." He tossed his hand facedown to the table.

Chance sighed to himself, a mental gust of relief. His cool blue eyes shifted to Calloway.

A nervous smile played over the blond man's lips when he tugged the wallet from his coat and opened it. "You've caught me in an awkward position, Mr. Sharpe. I seem to be a mite short. If you'll give me a few moments, I'll go to my stateroom and retrieve the funds needed to call your wager."

Before Chance could answer, the dealer spoke up: "I explained the house rules when you took your seat, Mr. Calloway, and you agreed to them. A man plays with the money he brings to the table—no loans, no IOUs. No exceptions to—"

"Surely Mr. Sharpe is willing to make an exception." Calloway's eyes were strangely dark orbs that seemed almost black when offset by his cottony blond hair. "All I asked is five minutes to return to my stateroom."

"Mr. Sharpe might be willing to make an exception, but I ain't!" The dealer once more interceded before the gambler could speak. "Rules is rules aboard the *Gulf Runner*. If you want to discuss 'em, talk with the captain. He's the one who made 'em."

A tinge of angry scarlet flushed Calloway's cheeks and neck. His eyes narrowed as he glared at the dealer and then at Chance. "Aren't you going to speak out, man? As one gentleman to another, I'm asking the leave of a few moments at most."

The gambler caught a slight shift of Calloway's right hand toward a bulge beneath the silk vest he wore. Chance's own right hand inched to the watch fob adangle from his vest pocket. No timepiece, but a double-barreled, .22 caliber derringer lay nestled in the pocket on the other end of the fob's gold chain. If Calloway tried for his hidden weapon, he'd find himself facing the derringer's two cocked hammers.

"Chance's silence is a gentleman's polite reply, Mr. Calloway." Tombaugh turned to his fellow poker player. "All of us agreed to the rules of this game as gentlemen. Now, as a gentleman, you are expected to abide by them."

A deeper red spread over Calloway's cheeks, but he didn't answer, except to glare at Chance, then push from the table and stride angrily across the riverboat's saloon.

He shoved through a single door at the forward portion of the narrow room to disappear into the night outside.

"Gentlemen, shall we continue?" The dealer pulled in the pot, took the house's one percent of the winnings and passed the rest to Chance. He then called for a fresh deck of cards and handed them to the gambler. "Your game and deal."

Chance broke the seal on the package of Riverboat No. 3's, tossed away the jokers, and began to shuffle. "Five card draw, no wild cards."

Tombaugh pulled in a pot that held a hundred of Chance's money. The gambler's mental ciphering tallied a total loss of two hundred since winning the big pot ten hands ago. He had given his fellow players ample opportunity to win back some of their losses. Easing from the table, he stood, said his goodnights, and then gathered his winnings.

"Tomorrow night, Chance?" Tombaugh asked while the gambler placed the bundle deep into his coat's inside pocket.

"I'll be here every night until we reach New Orleans," Chance answered. Once more bidding the players a goodnight, he turned and walked toward a mahogany bar in the forward portion of the riverboat's main cabin, or saloon as it was called more often than not.

The weight of his winnings—a grand total of twelve hundred for the evening—felt good. *And a damned bit more substantial than Indian gold!* He smiled, recalling his brother Wyatt and their recent, wild chase across the desert Southwest in search of one of the legendary seven cities of Cibola. In truth, they had found the gold, only to lose it beneath a collapsing mountain.

Chance shook his head. The fates ordained that riches of gold were meant for other men. Fortune, if it were to be his, waited at the gaming tables.

Reaching the bar, he ordered two fingers of straight bourbon. His gaze traveled around the narrow saloon as he sipped the whiskey. Even a steamer as small as the *Gulf*

Runner had a certain grandeur that could not be denied—the crystal chandeliers, the polished walnut tables, the flowing gowns of ladies who danced to the lively strains of a banjo band at the rear of the saloon.

All of which awoke an ache deep in his breast—a desire to once again stand on the decks of his own paddle-wheeler, the *Wild Card*. Something that would be denied him for at least another month, maybe two. The elegant sidewheeler was currently undergoing major repairs after a run-in with a gunboat four months ago.

The sound of laughter intruded into the gambler's thoughts. His head turned toward a group of men and women crowded around a table to his right. Again they broke out in laughter; tears streamed down several cheeks and more than a few of the congregated clutched at their sides.

Chance arched an eyebrow in the bartender's direction and tilted his head toward the crowd.

"Go take a listen for yourself," the bartender answered. "I've been catchin' a little here and there for the past hour. We got us a mighty funny storyteller aboard this trip downriver. Folks seem to enjoy his yarns about California an awful lot. He'll help make the time go a little faster."

The barkeeper's explanation provided little information. Moving to the opposite end of the bar in hope of glimpsing the entertaining gentleman at the table, Chance took another sip of the bourbon. He held the liquor's warmth in his mouth for a moment before letting it trickle down his throat. The change in position didn't help; passengers stood packed too closely around the man.

The outburst of laughter began to die, and with a sense of dramatic timing, a voice began, "As all of you can well imagine Jim Smiley was a mighty perplexed man. He just stood there scratchin' at the top of his head and starin' down at Dan'l . . ."

Jim Smiley? Dan'l? Chance straightened; both names scratched around at the back of his mind. They were so familiar, but he couldn't recall why.

"He ketched that frog by the back of the neck and hefted him . . ."

Dan'l was a *frog!* A distant smile touched Chance's lips. He had first heard the yarn of Jim Smiley, a man who was willing to wager on just about anything that struck his fancy, back in the days of the California gold rush. A friend of his in San Francisco had put the celebrated, wild tale down on paper and had it published in one of that city's newspapers under the title of "Jim Smiley and His Jumping Frog." That same friend recently published a volume of humorous stories and essays, and the yarn was included as "The Notorious Jumping Frog of Calaveras County."

"Smiley turned that frog upside down, and he belched out a double handful of quail shot . . ."

Chance's head cocked to one side. For the first time, he listened to the voice spinning the tale of that now notorious jumping frog contest. The gambler's smile widened. *It can't be!*

"Smiley set Dan'l down and lit after that feller, but he never ketched him!"

The enthralled audience broke into laughter as the speaker concluded the outrageous narrative. Chance tossed down the remainder of his drink and stepped to the crowd's edge. He could just make out the thick mat of auburn hair covering the top of the man's head.

"Bravo!" "Take a bow." Men and women called out as they clapped their delight. "How's about another one?" "The evening's young. Give us another tale."

The speaker pushed from the edge of the table on which he sat and took an exaggerated bow. When he righted himself, Chance got a full look at his face. The gambler grinned. "Why not tell these good ladies and gentlemen how your mother always said that you were born to be hanged, if someone didn't up and kill you first, Sam?"

The crowd's gaiety diminished to a hushed whisper of indignation and doubt the moment the gambler's question was uttered. Along the river, such an accusation was reason for fighting more often than not. The passengers inched back, opening a path between gambler and story-teller.

For the batting of an eyelash the heavy mustache that drooped below the corners of the speaker's mouth dipped even lower, and a shadow of doubt crossed his face. His teeth clamped firmly into the cigar he smoked. In the next instant an impish gleam flared from deep within his eyes. He scanned the faces of his audience. "Someone here knows more about my past than I usually let on."

"I think your ma was right," Chance continued, barely able to contain the stern poker face he wore. "Don't be-lieve I've ever seen a neck that looked as perfectly made to be stretched."

The speaker's eyes found Chance. Those eyes narrowed with a vague hint of recognition. "Stranger, those are words my own ma might have spoken, but I don't want these people to get the wrong idea about my mother. She's a gentle woman; she always warms the water in the bucket before she drowns the kittens."

A nervous chuckle ran through the passengers that said they were still uncertain of the situation.

The speaker's head moved from side to side as he stared at the gambler. "I've the distinct feeling you and I have met before."

A smile uplifted the corners of Chance's mouth. "The coldest winter I ever spent—"

"Was a summer in San Francisco," the man said, finish-ing the sentence he had often bemoaned years ago when he and the gambler had shared a beer or five in San Fran-cisco's saloons. Full recognition brought his eyes saucer wide. "Chance—Chance Sharpe? Is that really you?"

"One and the same, Sam Clemens." Chance's smile wi-dened to an ear-to-ear grin. "And if you keep spinning yarns like the one you just filled the ears of these gentle people with, someone *is* going to hang you."

The man returned the grin. "I won't argue that." He turned to his audience and said, "Ladies and gentlemen, I appreciate your kind attentiveness, but now I must bid you a good evening while I renew an old friendship with a rogue from my questionable past."

His words put the crowd at ease. One woman in a yellow dress said as he stepped toward the gambler, "We'll let you off tonight, Mr. Twain, but we'll be waiting for more stories tomorrow evening."

Sam Clemens's hand firmly grasped Chance's extended right hand. "Chance, I still find it hard to believe it's really you."

TWO

Sam Clemens drew heavily on his cigar and exhaled a cloud of blue smoke. He shook his head and laughed. "Stretching my neck! Lord, if there's anyone who I thought would end up wearing a rope necktie, it was you! That was if you didn't go and get yourself killed in President Lincoln's war!"

Chance smiled, recalling his friend's recounting his own brief stint as an officer who wore the Confederate gray. After an ankle injury, Clemens had given up his commission and traveled westward, eventually making his way to San Francisco where he wrote for the *Morning Call*, using the pen name *Mark Twain*. "You Johnny Rebs were more interested in sending me to my reward with a lead ball rather than a lynch rope, Sam. I barely managed—"

"Mr. Twain?" A young woman with blonde ringlets of curls piled atop her head walked to Clemens's side. She batted her blue eyes shyly and held out a book and a pencil. "I truly enjoyed your talk this evening, and I was hopeful that you would inscribe this for me."

"Excuse me for a moment, Chance." Clemens smiled and shrugged, took the book and pencil, and asked the woman her name.

"Polly, Polly Fuller," she replied in a demure tone barely above a whisper. "My favorite is the story you told tonight—the one about Jim Smiley and his frog Daniel."

The gambler recognized the volume—*The Celebrated Jumping Frog of Calveras Country, and Other Sketches*. Chance had purchased the book last year, and had they

10

now stood aboard his paddlewheeler, he would have led his friend to the library in his stateroom and requested a similar inscription in his own copy of Clemens's only book.

When Polly Fuller finished thanking the writer for his autograph and quietly walked away clutching the book to her bosom, Clemens turned back to Chance. "I'd like to say that I'm sorry about the interruption, but I'd be lying. I've only had a few people ask for me to sign my John Hancock to that book, and I'm not going to deny that I like it." He paused to glance over a shoulder. "Now, before a New York literary critic suddenly appears and tears his copy into confetti before my eyes, why don't we step outside for a breath of fresh air? Somebody's stunk up this saloon with a cheap stogie." He took another puff from his cigar to emphasize his point.

"'Mr. Twain'?" Chance asked as they walked from the *Gulf Runner*'s main cabin via the forward doors. "Both the bartender and your admirer back there called you 'Mr. Twain.' Are you going by *Mark Twain*, now?"

The writer propped his elbows on the deck's railing and gave another shrug. "Seem to be, although it's by no well-planned and thoroughly thought-out scheme of my own. It's just sort of happening."

Chance stared across the bow of the sternwheeler into the warm Mississippi summer night. He chuckled. "Now that leaves me in a bit of a quandary as what to call you."

"As long as the name doesn't profane my mother or father or our family ancestry, I'll probably answer to it." Clemens sucked in a deep breath and grinned. "You don't know how good it feels to be here, Chance. I've been away from this river for far too long. I was a pilot once—a *prima donna* of the Mississippi if there ever was one— dandified from stem to stern."

"Remember you mentioning that once or a thousand times," Chance replied. "The name Mark Twain came from the river."

"Mark twain—a leadman's call for two fathoms—safe

water. That's what it means, but that ain't exactly where I picked up the moniker."

The gambler arched a questioning eyebrow. "It isn't?"

"Actually, I kind of stole it from another pilot," Clemens answered with a hint of shame in his voice, "back when I was apprenticing for my pilot's license before the war. There was this old pilot, Isaiah Sellers by name. Well, Captain Sellers frequently wrote more than somewhat pompous letters to New Orleans newspapers. He'd jot down everything from his predictions of river conditions to his recollections as far back as 1811. He usually signed these 'Mark Twain.'"

Clemens paused, staring in the distance as though looking back to those days on the river before the Civil War. "In '59, I wrote a preposterous burlesque of Sellers's letters, detailing an impossible journey made in 1763 with a Chinaman as captain and a crew of Choctaw Indians. The *True Delta* published it. My young pilot friends and I thought it was nothing short of a masterpiece of wit."

He took another puff from the cigar, breathed a sad sigh, and shook his head. "What I hadn't reckon on was the effect my burlesque would have on Captain Sellers. When he read it, it broke his literary heart. He never wrote another word. I've always regretted that bit of tomfoolery."

The gambler said nothing, hearing the remorse in his friend's voice.

"When I headed West after the war broke out, I got myself a job on a newspaper in Virginia City. It was about that time I learned that Captain Sellers had died. I chose 'Mark Twain' for a *nom de plume* as my way of making up for what I did to that old man." Clemens looked at his friend. "Besides, what with him six-foot under and all, he didn't have any more use for it, and I did!"

Chance did a mental double take, uncertain whether Clemens's recounting of the 'Mark Twain' story was true or merely another yarn the writer had fabricated out of thin air. The gambler suspected there was more than a grain or two of truth in the recounting, in spite of Clemens's levity at the end. Humor often hid truth in its heart.

"What happened to you after I left San Francisco?" Chance drew a saber cigar from his coat and lit it. "The police were a mite hot under the collar about your attacks on their corruption."

"Enough that they stirred up a hornet's nest at city hall, and brought a libel suit against my newspaper—all of which doubled circulation." The writer chuckled to himself. "The police issued a summons for me, with an execution against all my personal effects. Before they could get their hands on me, a friend yanked me out of town and hid me away in a mining camp in the Tuolumne Hills. Tried my hand at running a hotel for a while. When things cooled off in San Francisco, I returned. Stayed there about a year until I received a commission from the *Sacramento Union* to sail to Hawaii and write about the islands, which I did for four delectable months—"

Hawaii, those Pacific Islands were but vestiges of exotic images in Chance's mind, places one read about, but never visited.

"—Then in '67, when Uncle Sam opened up travel to Europe again, I sailed to the Old World to do a series of articles on a group of American pilgrims' excursion to the Holy Land," Clemens continued. "Which is what brings me aboard this riverboat. I'm on my way to California to clear up some copyright problems with those articles. I have a publisher who wants to collect them in a book. I couldn't resist standing on the decks of a paddlewheeler again. It'll take a few weeks longer to get to the West Coast by this route, but it's worth it—every minute of it."

"Another book?" Chance smiled and shook his head. "You're going to disappoint your mother, Sam, if you go and make something out of yourself rather than getting hanged."

It was Clemens's turn to laugh. When the last of his chuckles subsided, he asked, "And what of yourself, Chance? How have you fared since abandoning the West?"

"In spite of myself, I managed to live through the war,"

the gambler replied. "The army kept me around for a year after Appomattox fighting Comanche and Kiowa in Kansas."

Chance gave no further details of his military service. While he believed in the Union blue that he had donned, war gave a man little to boast of. Gore, not glory, was the mainstay of battle.

"Within a week of my release, I was back on the river. In fact, I managed to win myself a riverboat in a poker game," the gambler related.

"A steamer?" Clemens's eyes widened with surprise. "This boat—the *Gulf Runner?*"

"No." Chance shook his head. "She's a sidewheeler named the *Wild Card* out of New Orleans. I'm not one to brag, but I'd hold her against the *Eclipse* for both style and speed."

"The *Eclipse!*" Awe touched the writer's voice as he repeated the name of that river legend. "Then why are we both standing here and not on the *Wild Card*'s decks? Damnation, man, I want to take a look at this floating palace of yours!"

"So would I," Chance replied. "Except the *Wild Card* ran into a bit of trouble with a gunboat."

"Gunboat?" Clemens's jaw sagged. "I thought you said you won this sidewheeler after the war?"

"I did. I did." The gambler held up both hands to fend off any more questions. "It's a long story, Sam, and my throat is feeling a mite parched."

"I've noticed the same feeling." Clemens rubbed a hand over his neck. "I think it's a common ailment among liars and their less honorable brothers—stretchers of the truth. Besides a few ounces of liquid refreshment will help lubricate the tongue. Something the both of us are going to need before we're through spinning the embellishments of our lives this night."

"How does a finger or three of Kentucky bourbon strike your fancy?" the gambler proposed.

"A gentlemen's drink, in spite of the fact that it's named after French royalty."

"I happen to know of a stateroom where an untouched bottle is neatly tucked away."

Clemens flourished an arm toward the entrance to the main cabin. "Lead the way, and I will follow."

"My room's the Virginia." Chance nodded toward the back of the long narrow saloon. "On the port side."

"Right next to my own stateroom," the writer said. "A pleasant coincidence, since I have to duck back in there and replenish my supply of cigars."

Chance caught the watchful shy eyes of Polly Fuller following them as they moved through the main cabin. "You still have the attention of a feminine admirer."

Clemens glanced at the young woman, smiled, and nodded. "Did you realize that as a boy I once worked for the very company that printed the volume she holds pressed so close to her abundant bosom?"

"John A. Gray and Green?" Chance said.

Clemens stopped abruptly and stared at his friend. "You *know* the firm who did the printing?"

"I bought a copy," Chance replied. "Even read it. Not bad for a man who was wanted by the San Francisco police department."

"My mother would have thought I was in good company," the writer said as they continued to their staterooms. "Give me a minute to get those cigars, and I'll join you."

Chance nodded. "No need to knock before you come in. I'll have a drink waiting for you."

As Clemens disappeared into his room, the gambler opened his own door and stepped inside. He froze!

Brad Calloway, whom he had faced at the poker table less than an hour ago, sat in a chair across the room. In his hand was an Army Colt, its barrel aimed directly at Chance's chest. "Won't you come in, Sharpe? We have some business to conclude."

Before Chance managed to answer, a man moved to the gambler's left, shooting out an arm to slam the door behind the gambler. The silent doorman had the look of a roust-about to him, as did the three toughs who stepped from the stateroom's shadows. Whatever Calloway had in mind, he had brought a small army with him to see that it was accomplished.

"Your streak of luck at the poker table tonight has left me in a rather embarrassing position." Calloway tugged back the Colt's hammer with the heel of his right thumb. "I don't want any trouble, but I will use this if necessary."

Chance held out both hands as he spoke. "Nor will you get any trouble from me. What is it that you want, Calloway?"

"For you to keep your arms exactly where they are at the moment to begin with, unless you want a slug of lead to mess up that ruffled shirt you're wearing." Calloway tilted his head toward the two men nearest the gambler. "Search him. He's carrying a belly-gun and probably another piece or two."

Chance silently cursed as the two men roughly freed the gun hidden beneath his vest and then found the derringer attached to the watch fob. He had lifted his hands to bring them closer to the weapons. Calloway had been ready for that.

"What do you want?" the gambler repeated.

"As I said, your luck at cards left me in an embarrassing position; I'm short of cash." Again Calloway nodded to the men at Chance's side. As they shoved the gambler across the room, Calloway stood, an amused smile playing across his lip. "I'm afraid that I have to relieve you of the bankroll you have inside your coat. Certain business associates of mine downriver aren't the type of men to understand gambling losses."

"Especially when it's their money that's been lost?" Chance asked.

"Perceptive." Calloway thrust an arm inside the gambler's coat and came out with the heavy wallet. He slipped the money into his own pocket and patted it. "There, that wasn't so difficult, was it? After all, it's only money. And what are a few dollars when a man's life hangs in the balance?"

Calloway's concept of a "few dollars" greatly differed from Chance's: there was over two thousand in the wallet. "What now?"

"A man as perceptive as yourself can surely recognize the awkward situation that would result should both of us remain aboard the *Gulf Runner*." Calloway's charcoal gray eyes darted to the men with him. "Which is why I employed these gentlemen to help alleviate the possibility of any ungainly accusations to the captain of this vessel that might arise from our little chat."

"So you kill me to eliminate the problem." Chance stalled for time. If he could keep this blond-haired weasel talking, he might—just might—find a way to extricate himself from between that well-known rock and a hard place. After all, all he had to do was overcome four human gorillas, and somehow manage to evade the Colt Calloway kept leveled at his chest. The odds weren't the greatest, he admitted, but they were all he had.

"I've no intention of killing you, Sharpe. Much too messy here, and there are far too many people aboard who would ask questions." A cold smile slid over Calloway's lips like oil spreading atop still water. "I'll let the river take care of you."

Calloway glanced at the two roustabouts standing at his sides and tilted his head toward the gambler. "Benny, Earl, get him out of here. I have no further need of this tinhorn."

Without so much as an acknowledging grunt, the two overmuscled apes in human clothing stepped forward with island-sized paws outstretched to snare their helpless prey. Chance's hands balled to white-knuckled fists. If he was to die this night, it would be with a fight.

"Chance, I just happened to find half a bottle of bourbon sitting beside my bed. I thought we might kill this old soldier before we started on your bottle." Sam Clemens opened the stateroom door and strode across the threshold.

The writer's entrance couldn't have been more perfectly timed if it had been carefully planned.

Chance's left arm swept out, slamming into Calloway's gun hand. The Colt flew from the man's grip as his arm jerked to the side. Simultaneously the gambler's right fist lashed out on a direct course to Calloway's nose.

He never made contact. Either Benny or Earl moved quicker; he was uncertain which. Something hard and cool slapped solidly against the side of the gambler's head.

In less time than it takes for a single heartbeat, the strength was sapped from every muscle in his body. On legs that went liquid and rubbery, he crumpled in a slow-motion turn. He tried to shake his head to escape the flashing, spinning meteor shower that streaked before his eyes. For an instant, his vision cleared—just long enough to see the two by the door slam it behind Clemens. The writer jerked around to face one of the gorillas, while the other applied a short length of lead pipe to the back of his skull. Clemens's lips kissed the stateroom's hardwood floor a split second before the gambler embraced the deck.

"Get 'em out of here," Calloway ordered, panic overriding his cool tone. "Be quick about it, dammit! Someone might have seen you hit him."

Chance tried to pick himself off the floor for a renewed assault against the weasel and his pet apes. His body refused to respond to his mental commands. He couldn't even force his eyelids to open. All he could do was lie facedown, floating in limbo somewhere between awareness and unconsciousness.

He didn't have to lift himself from the deck; Calloway's toughs did it for him. Two of them—he felt their rough hands clamp around his arms—rudely jerked him upward. Through the buzzing grayness that filled his head, he heard the stateroom's window open and the hurried scuffle of booted feet.

"Okay, it's clear. Get 'em out here," Calloway urged.

Like a stolen rag doll in the hands of two bullies, the gambler felt himself being shoved through the window and lowered to the walkway outside. Again he tried to break free of the well of semiconsciousness that had swallowed him. He couldn't; it was easier to just lie there.

"And the other one." Calloway's urgent voice intruded. "He got a good look at me."

Chance supposed the muffled sound he heard beside him was the unconscious Sam Clemens being dropped to the boiler deck's guard way. He really didn't care. It was hard enough to pull his errant thoughts together enough to be concerned about himself.

"Hurry." It was Calloway and his agitated voice again. "Get both of them overboard."

Chance could understand why the blond weasel would want to hasten his army of gorillas. If any passengers taking a late-night stroll happened upon the scene, it would be damned difficult for him to explain why he and the apes were playing with two unconscious men. Of course, Benny and Earl and their two other friends could always employ the pipes they carried and add to the bodies on the deck. Four or six men to dump into the Mississippi were only a little more trouble than two.

Again rough hands found the gambler's arms, fingers digging into his flesh. This time there was a difference; there were hands about his ankles, too! Two of the toughs, maybe all four, he couldn't be sure, lifted him from the deck. For a moment he felt himself being swung back and forth, then the hands released him.

He sensed motion—his useless body flung outward over the boiler deck rail into the Mississippi night. And there was the sensation of falling. Somewhere in the swirling maelstrom of his thoughts, he knew that he plummeted toward the inky river below, but all that mattered was that Calloway and his gorillas had finally left him alone.

THREE

Chance didn't hear his body strike the water. He *did* feel the river's coldness engulf him, seeping into his mouth and nose. An even greater coldness—the fear of certain death unless he shattered the numbing fist of unconsciousness clenched around his brain—brought him back to the land of the living.

Unreasoning fear did not rule his mind when his eyes opened to the watery blackness sucking him downward: the fear that scrambled clear thought was solidly rooted in logic. If he didn't do something damned quick, he was going to drown. That was reason enough for any mind to panic.

In desperation to survive, Chance's arms flailed against the current. His legs kicked out in an attempt to find non-existent footing. Neither action produced the results he hoped for. He remained beneath the water, unable to tell whether he moved toward the surface or propelled himself toward the Mississippi's muddy bottom.

Immediately he went motionless, waiting. His natural buoyancy moved him toward the river's surface. He then used his arms and legs to get him there with the true determination of a drowning man.

He came from beneath the water spitting and coughing and gulping for air. In spite of the night's mugginess that air felt cool and invigorating as it filled his lungs. His head jerked around as he attempted to locate his position. The low-riding hull of the *Gulf Runner* sliced through the river ten feet away.

He could almost reach out and touch the boat.

Almost. Calloway and his trained apes stood on the steamer's main deck to make certain that he didn't. None of the five appeared happy to see his head bobbing in the water. Calloway lifted his recovered Colt and took aim at the gambler. He frowned, then lowered the weapon, apparently realizing that a shot would draw attention to the very act he was trying to conceal. Chance was grateful for that; he was certain that he looked every bit the sitting duck, and would have been just as easy to drill with a piece of lead.

A sputtering series of hacking coughs that echoed his own of a moment ago came from his left. Sam Clemens's head shot above the water.

"Sam, here!" the gambler called as he swam toward his friend. "I'm over here."

"Well, I'm over *here!*" The writer's arms splashed against the current as he slowly turned in the water, apparently trying to find his own bearings. He noticed Chance and the *Gulf Runner* at the same time. "Come on, we can make it back aboard!" He then noticed Calloway and his overgrown primates disguised as men. "The bastards!"

Aboard the paddlewheeler, Calloway grinned like a cat who had just eaten the canary and then had a bowl of goldfish for dessert. He had noticed something that neither Chance nor the writer had seen—both men were rapidly being sucked toward the riverboat's single stern wheel. In a matter of seconds the massive, churning paddles would finish the job the lead pipes had started. Pipes or paddlewheel, it didn't matter. One gambler and one young writer would be so much flotsam floating facedown in the river.

"Dive!" Chance shouted the instant he recognized the cause of Calloway's sudden change in humor.

One glance at the turning wooden wheel was all it took for Clemens to do exactly what the gambler suggested. At Chance's side he ducked beneath the water and swam for the dark deeps.

When the gambler had first met a younger Mark Twain in San Francisco he had heard the then-newspaper man describe a riverboat as nothing more than a big raft with a hundred thousand dollars worth of jigsaw work nailed onto it. Anyone who was familiar with riverboats understood his meaning. A paddlewheeler was an opulent palace of fancy woodwork atop a shallow, almost flat hull that rode 90 percent above the water. It was this very fact that saved their lives.

Fighting against the current that sucked them toward the churning paddles, they reached a depth twelve feet below the surface, clearing the massive wheel with at least a foot to spare. Then the paddle-stirred current threw them out away from the riverboat. They kicked upward, breaking the surface beside one another.

"Next time you invite me for a social drink, please let me know whether you'll be having other guests." Clemens's arms and legs worked to keep his head above the water while he watched the *Gulf Runner* steam southward, leaving them in the middle of the Mississippi.

Chance didn't bother with an answer. In slow, steady strokes, he began to swim for the silhouette of a bank in the distance.

To those who made their living on America's waterways, the wild and treacherous Missouri River was known as the Big Muddy. The Mississippi earned the name the Father of Rivers. That title did not stem from the fact that it was a small, mild, easygoing stream of water that trickled through America's heartlands. In spring, summer, fall, or winter, whenever rains swelled the currents, the Mississippi overflowed its banks and spread its domain for two miles from side to side. Even under less savage conditions the river stretched for a mile in breadth.

For Chance Sharpe the Mississippi might have been a hundred miles wide. Mentally he realized that he had but a mere half mile to cross before he reached dry land. Physically, it seemed like a league or ten. In spite of easy, rhythmic strokes, he could swim no more than two or three minutes before he had to roll to his back and float while he regained the strength for another couple of minutes of progress toward the still distant bank.

"We'll make the shore by Independence Day or Christmas if we're lucky. A testament to the speed of river travel!" Sam Clemens grumbled from where he drifted on his own back fifteen feet to the gambler's port. "While I readily admit that I have an undying love for the Mississippi, this wasn't the method I had in mind for traveling it."

The best Chance could manage was a noncommittal grunt. His head throbbed painfully from a knot the size of a goose egg on the side of his skull—a souvenir with which to remember Benny and Earl. He still wasn't sure which of Calloway's pet animals had gifted him with the lump, but he dearly hoped to learn the answer to that pounding problem one day so that he might return the favor. Better yet would be to show Calloway the same courtesy.

"Chance, if it's not too ungentlemanly of me to inquire," Clemens said, "do you happen to know why your friends tried to take off the top of our heads? There's the distinct possibility that I am going to drown this night, and I would like to know why."

"They're not my friends. And nobody is going to drown." The gambler's tone was little more than his previous grunt. "Calloway wanted back the money he lost tonight and decided to take it."

Chance rolled over in the water, ready to try for the bank once again. His right arm was halfway into its beginning stroke when the flicker of light caught his eye. "Sam! Something's coming downriver."

"What?" The writer's head twisted to the right. "I see it! What is it—a skiff? Damned if that doesn't look like a camp fire floating atop the water."

Although it didn't make sense, that's exactly how the light appeared to Chance. It didn't matter. Lights meant men. The gambler began to shout. "Here! Over here! Men in the water!"

Clemens took up the call, bobbing up and down in the river as he alternated between waving at the approaching craft and trying to tread water. Half the words he cried were little more than watery sputters and gurgled gasps.

Whether it was Sam's effective combination of sounds that imitated the wails of a drowning man or the mere fact that the people aboard the craft were startled by hearing anything on the river at this late hour, Chance didn't know. But someone lit a lantern and held it high in the air to cast its light upon the inky water. The gambler shouted again, then began to swim toward the pale circle of light thrown by the oil lantern.

"Who's that?" a distinctive Negro voice questioned cautiously. "I hears ya, but I don't see nothin'."

"It's men, Odell." The answering voice was younger with high-pitched tones that might belong to a boy. "Can't you hear 'em a-callin' for help? They's drownin'!"

"Ain't no *men* on the river this time of night," the black answered. "Only haints on the river at this dark hour, I tell ya."

"Well, *we* ain't no haints, and *we're* on the river," the second voice replied with a touch of exasperation. "Hoist that light higher. They sound close."

"That's what's got me worried," the black said with decided uncertainty.

"Here to your starboard." Chance swam into the faint glow. "We're over here. There's two of us."

The gambler could make out the craft and the two aboard her. It was a simple raft—or what appeared to be a portion of what had once been an immense logger's raft that had broken away in a storm. The black was a large, barefooted man, wearing a white shirt, suspenders, and dark breeches. The owner of the second voice was a boy no more than fifteen at best with a thick, rumpled shock of red hair.

"I see ya!" The boy pointed to the swimming gambler and writer. "Keep your heads up, and I'll throw ya a rope."

"I tell ya, it ain't right to find no men swimmin' in the Mississip this time of night." The black man stuck out an arm to stop the youth.

The boy dodged the outstretched hand, lifted a coil of rope from the raft, and sent one end sailing out across the water. "Grab hold, and we'll haul ya in."

Chance and Clemens did just that while the black and boy began tugging them toward the raft, then helping them aboard. At least, the boy helped the two atop the lashed logs. The black man stepped back and stood beside a makeshift tent that was raised near the rear of the craft. He clutched at a leather pouch strung about his muscular neck on a braided rawhide cord.

"You two hunker up close to the fire here." The boy waved them closer to the flames with a hand while he tossed several pieces of dried driftwood onto the fire. He then turned to the black. "Odell, don't just stand there mutterin' to that hair ball of yours. Duck inside the tent and fetch these men the blankets 'fore they ketch their deaths. Can't you see by the fancy duds they're wearin' that we done fished royalty out of this river?"

"Royalty?" Odell didn't move a muscle, but kept both eyes glued to Chance and Clemens. The fingers of his right hand remained firmly locked about the mojo bag he wore.

"Jest look at their clothes and ya can tell!" The boy grinned proudly while his gaze shifted from his companion to the two men huddled by the blaze. "Ever seen men more duded up than these two—even grown men dressed for a Sunday prayer meetin'? Ya can tell by the cut of their clothes that these ain't ordinary folk, but blue-blooded royalty."

Chance stripped away his soggy coat and began to unbutton his vest. It would take hours for his clothing to dry by the heat cast from the jury-rigged firebox. There was nothing that said his skin had to be soaked for that time.

Beside him, Clemens carefully extracted five water-swollen cigars from a coat pocket and reverently positioned them before the dirt-lined firebox. He looked up and winked at the gambler. "If it doesn't come a shower tonight, we might be able to resurrect one of these by morning."

"How much them stogies cost, your royalty?" The boy pointed to the line of cigars. "Bet at least a nickel a piece —no twofers—for a highness."

The writer chuckled while he tugged off his own coat. "Each of these water-soaked, Cuban logs of tobacco costs four bits on the streets of New York City, lad—when a man is fortunate enough to locate them."

"Fifty-cent seegars and fancy duds like they's wearin'—they can't be nothin' but royalty, Odell." The boy's chest swelled as he waved a hand to the men he had rescued. "That one there is a duke and the one with the four-bit stogies gotta be a king at least."

"Duke?" Chance snorted and grimaced, glancing at his hand-tailored black suit and ruffled silk shirt. Obviously clothes didn't make the man when it came to this red-headed lad. Clemens wore a brown off-the-rack suit that sagged a bit at the shoulders, and his linen shirt appeared more yellow than white. And Clemens had been given the title of "king"!

"Breeding always tells, you Kentucky bumpkin!" The writer grinned, obviously reveling in the higher station in life the youth had arbitrarily assigned him. "It now becomes clear that mere gambling debts are not to blame for our misfortune, but that we were the beguiled victims of an assassination plot."

"King?" Chance snorted again.

"Royalty?" Odell's right hand relaxed, and he took a step forward. "You certain? They could be haints. Ain't neither one of us actually touched one."

"They ain't ghosts. See?" The boy stepped beside Clemens, reached down, and pinched the flesh of his now bare upper left arm between thumb and forefinger.

The writer yelped at the unexpected side attack and jerked his arm away.

Chance grinned. "There seem to be certain benefits of being only a lowly duke."

"A ruler always sits atop a shaky throne." The writer vigorously rubbed at his arm.

The boy faced Odell again. "What did I tell ya! Flesh and blood jest like me or you—only their blood's blue where ours is common red. Now fetch them blankets. An ya might get the coffee and maybe some of that dried beef. Drownin' always leaves men hungry."

"And yourselves?" Clemens asked, wiping his fingers on the knees of his semi-dried pants as he concluded an abbreviated version of their abrupt disembarking from the *Gulf Runner*. "By the way, could I have another slice of that bread and perhaps a small portion of the beef? Oh, and another cup of coffee?"

Both the boy and the black immediately snapped to and filled his requests.

The gambler noted that his friend made no attempt to correct the boy's misconception that they were of royal blood during his recounting of their being thrown overboard. If anything, he seemed to enjoy being called "your kingship" and "your kingness." Nor did Clemens, who gave his name as "Mark Twain" and frowned when Chance called him "Sam," seem to mind that his rescuers waited on him hand and foot.

"I believe that I had inquired as to you two," Mark Twain said as Odell and the boy settled across the fire from them.

"Me, I's on my way to New Orleans to look for my wife, Thelma, and my son, Clyde. Both was sold down the river 'fore the war broke out," Odell said, taking a long drink from his own coffee cup. He explained how a preacher and his wife in Missouri had written letters for him after the war, and they had learned that his family had ended up in the Crescent City. However, neither the woman or child could be located. "I decided to go fetch 'em home myself. Ain't no white man gonna pay that much attention to a nigger's troubles. If a man wants something done, he's got to do it himself."

"Instead of wastin' good money on a riverboat, Odell here ketched a ride downriver on this fine raft of mine." The boy waved both arms outward to indicate the expanse of the raft.

"Don't go lying to no royalty," Odell admonished the youth. "Ain't neither of us got more'n a few coppers to our names."

"And you?" Clemens tilted his head toward the boy. "I don't remember even hearing the name of the brave young man who saved our lives."

"Tuck, your kinghood—Tuck Finn." The boy's chest expanded to twice its usual size as he spoke the name. "This here's my raft, and I'm on my way downriver to join my father, Mike Finn. Maybe you heard of him?"

"Finn? I don't recall the name." Clemens shook his head. "Have you heard of a Michael Finn, Chance?"

The gambler swallowed a mouthful of coffee before he could answer. "Don't reckon I have."

A shadow of disappointment darkened the youth's face, and his chest deflated. "Neither of you have heard of Mike Finn, King of the River? I can't believe it! Every man, woman, and child in this God-fearing nation has heard of Mike Finn. He's the greatest flatboat man ever to work the Mississippi. With a crew of three men, he can haul more cargo in one flatboat than any two steamers—and in half the time. He's a livin' legend, and me, I'm his only son!"

"Mike Finn?" Clemens glanced at the gambler with a questioning eyebrow arched to his hairline. "Are you certain you don't mean Mike Fink, lad? Mike Fink, who he himself spelled his name M-i-c-h-e P-h-i-n-c-k."

"That what I said, Fink," the boy hastily replied. "Tuck Fink, son of Mike Fink."

"Then I have heard of him." The writer played out a bit more line. "Mike Fink, the greatest keelboater to ever ride the Mississippi or Missouri—"

The beaming smile returned to the boy's face, and his head nodded eagerly.

"That's *keelboat,* lad. Not *flatboat!*"

"Flatboat? Did I say flatboat?" The boy's head shot up. "Must have been a slip of the tongue, what with a keelboat and a flatboat being so much alike, you know."

"About alike as what goes in one end of a bull and what

comes out the other." Clemens squinted both eyes and stared at the redheaded youth. "I'd make you between thirteen and fifteen. Just about the right age for a runaway apprentice."

The boy's eyes lowered as though he were embarrassed. His head nodded wearily. "I'm a-feared ya've found me out. That's exactly what I am, your kingship. My name's George Peters. After my ma and pap died, my aunt 'prenticed me to a farmer north of Hannibal, Missouri, name of Claybourne. For two long years, I served him like a son would serve a father."

Chance listened as George Peters—if that really was his name, and the gambler won't have staked a dime bet on it—unfolded a tale that compounded the trials of Job with every hardship that had befallen the heroes in the novels of Charles Dickens. The labors Claybourne had required of the lad would have broken the backs of a hundred strong men, and the suffering and hardships the boy had endured would have shattered the hearts and souls of another thousand.

If they had occurred, which, of course, they hadn't. There was no man who walked the earth who would have believed even a portion of George Peters's fabrication. Chance didn't, and it was obvious that Clemens didn't either. However, the writer seemed totally enthralled with every lie the boy artfully wove. Clemens sat straight and hung on each word George Peters uttered—and he uttered enough to fill at least a volume or two.

After the first half hour, the gambler could take no more. His thoughts returned to the river they slowly drifted down. Both were totally without money and a long way from the delta country. Clemens's five water-logged cigars represented the only possessions either man had in his pockets. Chance did have a stiletto sheathed inside the top of his right boot, but the small knife would go about as far as the cigars would in buying them passage aboard a riverboat.

FOUR

Chance groaned, rolled to one side, and threw an arm over his face. It didn't help, the insistent light still found a way to his eyes. He shifted to his opposite side and tried the other arm. The situation offered no improvement. The gambler flopped to his back and opened both eyes to slits.

Morning? He blinked against the soft pastel yellow of the summer morning. *The sun can't be up yet!* But there was no way to deny the warm glow that illuminated the world.

He groaned again. It seemed like mere minutes had passed since he had stretched out atop the log raft and tried to sleep. After an eternity or two of twisting and rearranging his body to locate a spot where the unforgiving logs didn't hold a personal grudge against his presence, he finally managed to drift off.

"Good morning!" a voice far too cheerful to greet the aches and kinks in the gambler's arms, legs, and back called out to him. "Have yourself a fine rest? The good Lord knows that you slept long enough!"

"Huh?" Chance pushed to his elbows, accompanied by a chorus of nagging pains from every inch of his body. A man who is accustomed to earning his livelihood during the night doesn't consider the day begun until it's half over. By the gambler's time it was still yesterday by several hours.

"I said that you slept the sleep of the dead," the voice answered, still sounding too cheery for the early hour.

Prying his reluctant eyes wider, Chance forced a stiff

30

neck to turn to the right and then to the left. He couldn't find the voice's owner.

"I was beginning to think you intended to sleep your way through this beautiful morning."

"I was *hoping* for the same thing," the gambler answered with as much sarcasm as he could muster. The sleep-dryness of his mouth completely dulled the edge to his tongue.

"It's mornings like this that make a man glad to be alive." The voice persisted in praising the glories of a new day when Chance's mind and body insisted it was still night.

However, the gambler did locate the direction from which the voice came—directly behind him. Stiff or not, his neck was not designed to twist around that far. With concerted effort, he managed to direct his arms and legs to work in unison and shift toward the voice. The rest of his body was dragged around for the ride.

Sam Clemens sat on the side of the raft with his pant-legs rolled above knobby knees and feet dangling in the river. He was bare-chested except for suspenders running over his shoulders. His thick drooping mustache was supported by a broad grin that stretched from ear to ear.

"While you've been sawing logs, I've been earning a living." He reached down and pulled a string of five catfish from the water. "These will make the tastiest breakfast you've ever sunk your teeth into."

For the first time the gambler noticed that his friend held a makeshift fishing pole cut from a river beech. "Fishing?" Chance attempted to keep disbelief from his voice; he wanted his tone to be more vicious than that. "Last night a blond weasel and his four pet apes tried to kill us and were successful in stranding us on this raft, and all you can do is sit there and fish?"

"It beats sleeping." The wide grin remained on the writer's face, a fact that only increased the gambler's irritation. "At least I'll put food in our bellies. What have you accomplished?"

If Clemens thought minor things like logic and facts were going to dissuade the gambler from his point of argument, he was mistaken. "Sam, I don't think you quite understand the position we're in. In case you haven't noticed, this isn't the *Gulf Runner*'s decks we're standing on."

"Sitting on," the writer corrected while he jerked his fishing pole up and pulled another catfish from the river. "That makes six."

Chance cursed under his breath. In spite of their common surroundings, his friend seemed to be dwelling in a totally different world, nor did the gambler understand exactly what world it was, although he was certain Clemens had every idiot in every village across the nation as his neighbors.

Drawing a deep breath to regroup his thoughts and find another route to approach the man, Chance glanced around the raft. Neither Odell nor George Peters were to be found.

"Where are the captain and crew of this mighty vessel?" the gambler asked, his gaze returning to Clemens.

"About daylight we pulled to the bank," Clemens replied, adding the sixth fish to his heavy string. He nodded westward. "Both of them headed out that way. Said they were going to forage for berries, persimmons, and wild plums."

"Persimmons and berries?" Chance glared at his friend. "You certain they didn't say roots and nuts? Sam, persimmons don't ripen until fall. This is the summer, remember? You certain they didn't get tired of all that kingshipping you had them doing last night and decide to run off?"

Idly the writer rose, walked to the bank, and used the end of the beech pole to dig around in the ground. After a few tentative probes, he stooped and came up with a worm between his fingers. He securely attached the writhing bait to his hook as he returned to the edge of the raft and once more perched on its edge.

"You know, Chance," he said while he let the worm sink beneath the water's surface, "you're taking the wrong outlook on all of this. Your friends back on the *Gulf Run-*

ner tried to kill us, that's true. It's also true that neither one of us has a penny in his pockets. But we aren't dead; we're very much alive and kicking. Back when we were a mite younger and hadn't gone full grown and hair all over, this was exactly the type of adventure we used to yearn for. And that's what it is, Chance, an adventure. You should think of it as that—a *great adventure!*"

Adventure? The gambler shook his head. Apparently Clemens and he had had different daydreams when they were boys. Chance had yearned to ride the decks of the riverboats that he used to watch. He had run away from his father's Kentucky farm at age thirteen to do just that.

"Take this raft, for instance." The writer's knuckles rapped against a log to draw the gambler's attention. "To you it might look like simple wood lashed together. But it's not. This is good hardwood, probably come downriver from way up on the Missouri. I'd say it's part of a logger's raft that was torn away on a snag or maybe a sandbar."

Chance rolled his eyes. He didn't need a lecture about logger rafts; he had recognized the raft as such last night.

"When I was a boy back in Hannibal, my friends and I used to borrow a skiff or a canoe—without its owner knowing, of course—and search the river for a prize such as this." Clemens's gaze moved over the raft. His eyes contained a distant look that said his thoughts traveled back to his childhood. "One salvaged log broke loose from a raft could bring as much as ten dollars. Did you realize that, Chance?"

The gambler's own gaze dipped to the logs on which he sat. Even at five dollars a log, the raft would bring fifty dollars. It might—just might—offer a solution to their problem.

"Sam, grown men don't sail the Mississippi on rafts, not unless they're loggers, which we aren't." Chance contained his irritation, and forced understanding into his tone. "Neither one of us can afford to spend the rest of the summer drifting with the current. You have to be in California to tend your new book, and I have a riverboat under repair in New Orleans."

Clemens looked past the gambler and stared at the river. For several moments he said nothing, then he drew a heavy breath and sighed. "You're right, of course. I have a boat to meet in New Orleans. I can't miss it." His gaze returned to his old friend. "You see, Chance, I've met a young lady in New York that I intend to marry. I can't do that until I improve my financial position, something this new book will do."

Chance smiled inwardly; apparently mentioning California had done the trick. "We need to find a town with a telegraph office, Sam. I can wire New Orleans and have my attorney send the funds needed to get both of us downriver."

The writer glanced back to the river; a hint of sorrow hung at the corners of his eyes. It was more than obvious that abandoning this "great adventure" wasn't easy for him. However, that was the price he paid for adulthood.

"When George and Odell come back, I'll talk with them," he finally said. "It shouldn't be too much trouble for us to put in at the next town we come to."

Chance stood and lifted his clothing from the raft. The morning sun had sucked the last of the river from them. He began to dress. "Why don't I gather some wood, and then we'll see about cooking that breakfast you promised."

"Sounds good to me." The sparkle returned to Clemens's eyes. "George and Odell should be back soon. They've been gone about an hour now."

Chance moved to the edge of the raft and jumped to the shore. Finding firewood proved to be a relatively easy task; the Mississippi kept a steady supply of limbs and boards washed against the banks. All the gambler had to do was collect it. His arms were laden with a heavy load of driftwood when he heard the first shout.

"Cast off the line! Shove off!"

In long strides Chance ran back to the raft and tossed down his load of wood. Clemens stood and peered into the woods, but shook his head when the gambler cast him a questioning look.

"Cast off!" the voice cried again. This time it was quite discernible. It belonged to George Peters, and the boy was obviously distressed.

"I'll get the line!" Clemens leaped to the shore and untied the single rope that moored the raft to the bank.

"Get the raft into the water!" Odell now shouted. "Get the raft into the water!"

Chance could see the black and the boy now. Both tore through the woods as though the demons of Hell were breathing down their necks. The gambler joined his friend on the bank and bent his back to the task of shoving off.

George and Odell broke from the woods, hit the water in a full run that sent water showering in the air, and scrambled onto the logs, grunting, panting, and squawking.

It was the squawking that jerked Chance's head around since the agitated cackle was not a sound he normally associated with either man or boy.

George clutched a plump red hen in his arms. He caught the gambler's gaze and grinned. "I thought it might be nice to have fried chicken for a change."

Chance began to understand the reason for the pair's distress. Chicken hens, red or any other color, weren't wild denizens of American forests. The hen had come from one place—a chicken coop! A fact that became all too apparent when an angry voice roared from the woods: "Come back here you sons of bitches! Get your asses back here!"

The owner was a red-faced farmer, who ran toward the shoreline with one hand upraised in a fist, and the other toting a double-barrelled shotgun.

"The river's movin' a mite sluggish this mornin'." Odell found a long pole near the rear of the raft and began poling the small craft away from the bank.

Chance felt the Mississippi's current catch the raft, drawing it out toward the center of the river. That his chicken thieves were beyond the range of his scattergun didn't stop the farmer from letting loose with both barrels when he reached the river. Quail shot peppered the water twenty feet short of the escaping raft.

Behind him George and Clemens laughed at the string of curses the farmer shouted after them, while Odell heaved a relieved sigh and the hen cackled. Chance merely groaned inwardly. Not only was he stranded aboard a raft without a penny to his name, but he had come damned near losing his life because of chicken thieves. In spite of the cloudless blue overhead, the morning didn't appear as bright as it had but moments before.

FIVE

George Peters was no more. As Chance licked the grease from his fingers—the only remains of three pieces of crisp, fried chicken, except for the bones, which he tossed overboard—George Peters abruptly became George Jackson.

The metamorphosis wasn't a difficult one. All it took was a few questions from silver-tongued Clemens and the redheaded youth once more hung chin to chest and owned up to his falsehoods. George Jackson claimed to have escaped from a Saint Louis orphanage.

"The state put me there after my ma and pap died of the pox," the boy said with the sincerity of a New Orleans street hustler. "I ran away two weeks back and am now searchin' for my Uncle Jake, who owns a farm in Arkansas. When I find him, he'll take me in as one—"

The gambler was spared the rest of the woeful tale; it started to rain. No mere summer shower this. Dark thunderheads blew in from the west in a matter of minutes to unleash torrents of wind-lashed rain. Lightning rent the sky, dancing from one horizon to the other like the legs of some unearthly beast of fire. Thunder boomed and rolled like cannons belching to defend the ramparts of heaven from Lucifer's unholy legions of the damned.

Chance and the others scrambled to escape the downpour. Alacrity was of no value. All four were soaked to the bone before they managed to jury-rig an extension to the tent and salvage the flickering flames of their fire. Then they huddled beneath the wind-popped canvas and stared forlornly out at the sheets of rain deluging the river.

"A gully-washer if I ever saw one," Odell said glumly.

"A flash-flooder," George Jackson added with an af-
firming nod.

"A frog-strangler," Clemens put in, continuing the one-
upmanship of a sudden disaster.

It was all these things Chance agreed, although he preferred his friend's description. After all, Clemens had once
been a riverboat pilot and was thus well acquainted with
the correct portions of doom and gloom required in one's
voice when discussing the weather. For a pilot sunshine
meant drought, and rain meant a flood to equal the one
Noah had so ably handled—although most pilots would
readily admit to being superior helmsmen to that Biblical
figure. Nor would they blush when they made the claim.

Gully-washer, flash-flooder, or frog-strangler—the
name was unimportant. It rained cats and dogs, maybe
horses and cows—for twenty minutes. Then the storm
played out and was replaced by a muggy drizzle and a fog
as thick as pea soup that seemed to be breathed to life from
the banks of the river itself.

The misty rain and fog remained on the Mississippi for
three days running. Neither man nor boy could do more
than guess at their position along the winding river. Although they kept close to the eastern bank to avoid the
paddlewheelers they heard picking their way up- and
downstream, their steam whistles constantly blasting out
warnings, they discerned no landmark that might suggest a
location. In truth, they only rarely glimpsed the bank, let
alone saw anything that could be remotely mistaken for a
landmark. Even when they moored, they remained close to
the raft for fear of getting lost in the dense fog that cloaked
the river.

The morning of the fourth day brought the sun. The last
vestiges of the fog burned off. Both Clemens and Chance
immediately recognized Wolf Island to the starboard. That
massive parcel of land split the Mississippi into wide

streams with the state of Missouri to the west and Kentucky on the east.

"This means we've slipped past Cairo in the fog," Clemens said, watching Wolf Island as the raft drifted past.

The gambler thought that was a perceptive observation on his friend's part, especially since Kentucky formed the eastern bank and Illinois was positioned north of Kentucky on every map and chart he had ever read. However, he kept any remarks concerning Cairo to himself. Instead he said, "There's a small town called Longway just downriver. We should reach it by early afternoon. They've a telegraph there."

Clemens nodded and assured the gambler that the raft would pull into Longway.

Actually the raft was moored half a mile south of the Kentucky town. George Elexander was afraid some wood-yard would claim the raft's logs to be theirs and confiscate the vessel. Chance felt the excuse an unlikely one, but he didn't contradict it. The raft did, after all, belong to the boy. Even Odell admitted that.

Yesterday George Jackson had revealed himself to be George Elexander as they had dined on bass and catfish Clemens had caught. The day before the redheaded youth had sworn his "true" name was George Tucker, and that he was the son of a rich railroad man and had run away to see the world. Or was he the only child of a New York heiress who had been kidnapped by gypsies? Chance found it increasingly difficult to keep the boy's names and stories straight.

He was, however, beginning to believe that George Peters-Jackson-Elexander's first name was George. Still, if it came down to brass tacks, he wasn't willing to wager on it.

While George and Odell went off to "scout the lay of the land," which the gambler supposed meant find another chicken coop to raid, he and Clemens straightened their clothes to make themselves as presentable as possible, which was wasted energy as far as Chance was concerned.

While the river and rain had kept his suit clean, he had been living in it for five days and its wrinkles now had wrinkles. So did the writer's clothing.

Longway's constable didn't think much of the two friends' presentability either. A man in his early fifties, he eyed the pair with suspicion as they walked into his office. With that same suspicion, he listened to their recounting of the encounter with Brad Calloway and his four toughs.

"Gentlemen," he said as they concluded their tale of misfortune, "it's obvious to me that you have been dealt more than your share of misjustice, but I'm afraid that there is nothing that I can do for you. Longway's coffers are almost bare, and there's been little enough funds to keep this town running since the war. If I could help you, I would. But as you can see, this matter is totally beyond the scope of my office."

Chance was fully intent on telling the constable exactly what he thought of the scope of his office when Clemens spoke up and allowed how he fully understood the man's predicament and thanked him for the courtesy of listening. The writer then nudged Chance toward the door to the office.

"Gentlemen," the constable called out as the door opened, "it is my duty to inform both of you that if I should happen to find either one of you, or both of you, in this town tomorrow, and if you are not gainfully employed, I will have to arrest you for vagrancy, fine you ten dollars, and lock you in that cell back there until you pay the fine."

Again Clemens thanked the man, and shoved the growling gambler outside, hastily closing the door behind them, barely sparing the constable the tirade of curses that spewed from Chance's lips. If the gambler expected sympathy from his friend, he was out of luck.

"What did you expect? Just look at you! Would you believe a bum who looks like you do?" Clemens shot Chance a reprimanding glance. "We're damned lucky he didn't throw us behind bars and toss away the key."

Snorting, Chance pivoted and stalked down the street

until he found a shingle that marked one of the town's storefronts as containing a telegraph within. Like the constable, the telegrapher seemed to be of a suspicious nature. In spite of a full retelling of the details of their plight, the man asked the gambler for three dollars to wire the message to New Orleans.

"If I had three dollars, I wouldn't be here." Chance's exasperation threatened to explode into another tirade. "If you'll read the message, you'll see that I'm wiring my attorney to send me funds."

The telegrapher read the message, acknowledged that it was exactly what Chance had said it was, and then said, "That will be three dollars, please."

"But we don't have three dollars!" The gambler's voice rose an octave. "If we had three dollars, I wouldn't be asking you to send the message and subtracting your bill from the money my attorney will wire here."

"No money, no telegram. This *is* a telegraph office, friend, not a bank giving out loans." The telegrapher shrugged, then scratched his chin. "You got anything else you could use for money—ring or something? I could accept that for a wire—until your money came, that is."

Clemens dug into his pockets, turning them inside out in a fruitless search for collateral. Likewise Chance came up empty-handed until he probed the left pocket of his coat. He grinned as he extracted a gold pocket watch that he had forgotten about.

"What about this?" He displayed the watch on the palm of a hand before the telegrapher. "Surely a man of your discriminating taste can see that this is worth more than three dollars."

The telegrapher's interest tripled as he lifted the watch and carefully examined it. He then thumbed it open. "It ain't runnin'! You ain't tryin' to pull a fast one on me, are you? I ain't got no need of a busted watch."

"It just needs winding," the gambler assured the man. "I haven't wound it in days."

The telegrapher quickly wound the watch. His frown

deepened; the timepiece's second hand remained motionless.

"Perhaps, if you shook it a bit," Clemens suggested.

The writer's well-meant suggestion was disastrous. The telegrapher did just that, and sent a spray of droplets into the air. Every one flew from the watch. Calloway's dunking in the Mississippi and three days of rain had worked their damage.

The telegrapher dropped the watch back into Chance's still open palm. "You two better get the hell out of here 'fore I send for the constable. He don't take kindly to confidence men in this town."

"The constable doesn't take kindly to having us in this town period," Clemens whispered as he shoved the gambler out the door of the telegraph office.

Which was probably the correct thing to do, because Chance had been seriously considering freeing the stiletto in his boot and seeing if the telegrapher would barter a telegram to New Orleans in exchange for keeping his throat in one piece.

"What now?" Clemens glanced around the small town. Except for a simple buggy drawn by a sleek chestnut, Longway's main street was empty.

"If I had a dollar, I'd buy you a drink," Chance said, absentmindedly nodding toward a saloon across the street. His thoughts were elsewhere, trying to decide what should be their next plan of action.

"An excellent idea!" The writer slapped his friend on the back and started for the saloon's swinging doors. "Charity is not normally an attribute one associates with the law, nor is it a courtesy extended by big business corporations. But find a man with a drink or two beneath his belt, and you will find a generous man."

"Or you'll find a man willing to rearrange your face for free," Chance answered as he followed his friend.

"You're being too hard," Clemens assured him. "It appears that the only way we're going to get the three dollars we need is to beg for it. If that's what it takes, then that's what we'll do."

"We could offer to work," Chance suggested.

Clemens didn't hear, or else ignored the words, as he pushed inside the saloon. Chance shook his head and walked through the double swinging doors after the writer.

"C'mon in, neighbors!" A thin, long-legged man standing at the rear of a long, dark-stained bar lifted an arm and waved to the newcomers. "Share a drink with us. We're celebrating the demise of the late Clem Shepherdson."

A bartender wearing a worried look poured two shot glasses abrim with amber bourbon. He walked to the end of the bar and slid the whiskey to Clemens and Chance. "You'd be wise to accept these and toast Shepherdson's death," he whispered. "It ain't healthy to do contrary."

Clemens didn't hesitate. He took the two drinks from the bar, handed one to the gambler, then turned to the lanky man who had hailed them when they entered. He lifted the bourbon to the man. "Friend, I appreciate your courteous gesture, and I offer a toast to the late Mr. Shepherdson's untimely demise."

The man at the end of the bar accepted Clemens's offered words and put back a fresh shot of bourbon in one hearty gulp. Both the writer and gambler sipped from their glasses.

"The name's Grangerford, Colonel Grangerford," the man said with a decidedly pleased smack of his lips.

Chance wouldn't hazard a guess as to the authenticity of the man's military title. Since the end of the war, it had become the vogue with Kentucky males, especially those among the landed gentry, to tack *Colonel* in front of their names like a martyr's badge to signify their undying support of a lost cause. Colonels in Kentucky came a dime for three dozen.

"However, Shepherdson's dying wasn't untimely." Grangerford chuckled. "If there's a truth to the matter, it was quite timely—in fact, just about two hours gone now. I know—I killed the lowborn snake in the grass."

Chance nearly choked on the bourbon that rolled down his throat. Clemens's eyes went saucer wide.

"When the whoreson back-shot my brother Jeff last spring, he rode into town and ordered a round for everyone in the house," Grangerford continued. "Today there'll be two drinks for everyone. It's a matter of gentlemanly honor."

It made perfect sense to the gambler. An honorable man couldn't allow a dead man to one-up him, especially if the deceased happened to be a man whose soul one had just sent to its eternal reward.

While Grangerford downed two more shots and elaborated on the more gruesome highlights of a ten-year feud between his family and the Shepherdsons—a private war that had cost the lives of twenty men, five women, and a handful of children in assorted sizes—Chance's gaze moved around the saloon. At least fifty men occupied the tables or stood along the bar, which was a surprisingly large assembly to find this early in the afternoon in a town as small as Longway. Either the men of the town had congregated at the call of free booze, or there was so little to celebrate in the hamlet that even the murder of a neighbor was reason enough for festivities.

Actually, the gambler was grateful for Grangerford's generosity, in spite of his dubious motive. The drink in hand meant he didn't have to reveal his lack of coin in pocket. The promised second drink made it doubly nice.

"Colonel Grangerford!" A man in worn overalls and a sweat-stained, floppy-brimmed hat burst through the swinging doors. "Colonel Grangerford, five Shepherdsons just drove into town in that green-lacquered buggy of theirs."

From the ashen hue that washed over the colonel's face, Chance knew that the celebration had come to an abrupt end. Grangerford swallowed hard—this time without bourbon to accompany the action. Hands atremble, he extracted two gold pieces from a jacket pocket and tossed them to the bar. "That's to cover the two rounds. See that everybody gets what's coming to them."

However, it was easy to tell that Grangerford was far more concerned with the possibility of his getting what was coming to him. He quietly slipped out of the saloon via a back door without waiting to say hello to the Shephersons or even offering to buy them a drink.

Less than a minute passed when the gambler heard the indisputable sound of horse hooves rapidly sloshing through the muddy streets outside. Apparently Colonel Grangerford had managed to reach his mount and was doing his best to make a hasty retreat before drawing the attention of the Shepherdsons.

It didn't work. Five rifles cracked. Chance listened, but he didn't hear a body hit the mud, nor did he hear a cheer rise from the throats of the Shepherdsons. Which meant Colonel Grangerford was a damned lucky man or the Shepherdsons couldn't hit the broad side of a barn. Either way, the tally of the ten-year-old feud would be increased by only one this day.

With a shrug, Chance turned back to the barroom, as did Clemens. After a silent moment of examining the men around the saloon, the writer nudged Chance's side.

"They don't seem too upset by Grangerford's departure, do they?" he whispered.

The barroom's clients hadn't glanced toward the doors when the shots had sounded outside. Chance's shoulders gave another shrug. "All of them already received their second round. We haven't."

Nor did the gambler expect the bartender to provide the drink Grangerford had paid for in advance. After all, how would the colonel ever know?

Chance had no more than completed the thought when the bartender poured two more shots and slid them across the bar to the strangers. "Here you go, men, compliments of Colonel Grangerford." The man then returned to his other customers.

For a moment Chance thought he had misjudged the

bartender's honesty. Then he realized the man had the beginning of a very profitable business opportunity taking
seed in town. If the one-upmanship continued with each
Shepherdson or Grangerford victory, the bartender would
be able to make enough to retire in a single night a few
bodies from now. Obviously he was protecting his interest
by supplying the two drinks. If word ever got back to either of the two families that he welshed on his obligations,
the Shepherdsons and Grangerfords might take their celebration business elsewhere.

As the gambler glanced around the barroom again, his
gaze alighted on a friendly game of poker underway in a
corner. He wistfully studied the pot of pennies and nickels
piled at the center of the table. It wasn't much, no more
than a dollar at best. However, he didn't need but three
dollars to send his telegram to New Orleans. With a dollar
stake, maybe even four bits, he could take a chair in the
game. Trouble was he didn't even have a penny.

"Let me see that watch of yours." Clemens held out a
hand, which closed around the water-logged pocketwatch
the gambler placed in it. "I believe that I have just discovered the means to remedy our poverty."

He didn't give Chance the opportunity to question him,
but crossed the saloon to two billiard tables on the far side
of the room. He dangled the useless gold watch in front of
two men holding cue sticks. For a moment the writer and
the two exchanged words, then Clemens was handed one
of the sticks.

Chance trembled inwardly. He had totally forgotten
about his friend's attraction to billiards. Seeing Clemens
arranging the colored balls on the green felt brought back a
flood of memories of similar bars in San Francisco when
the writer had spent hour upon hour playing billiards.
Those visions reawoke another memory—a ninety-year-
old man with rheumatism in all ten fingers could shoot
better than the writer!

Chance's tremble of doubt transformed into a shiver of

fear when the clack of breaking balls sounded over the din of barroom conversation.

Clemens's opponent missed his first shot, and the writer used his stick to point to a corner. He looked awkward as he bent over the table and sighted on a ball. His stick pumped back and forth a couple of times, then he neatly sent the cue forward, which in turn solidly smacked into his chosen ball. A feat that surprised the gambler. More amazing was the fact that the ball smoothly bounced off two of the table's cushions and rolled neatly into the selected corner.

Apparently Clemens had practiced since their last meeting in San Francisco, because from that point on, the writer controlled the game. He commanded stick, cue, and balls with the touch of a master. For his effort, his opponent placed a two-bit piece on the table, then threw another down in challenge. Clemens collected a second coin fifteen minutes later.

Nor was that the last of the men challenging his craft. For as little as a nickel or as much as fifty cents, Longway's men lined up to try their skill against the billiard wizard who visited their town. And those who didn't feel their ability great enough to take a shot at dethroning the new king of the billiard table, gathered around cheering on each local challenger who took up the cue stick of battle.

Chance watched from the bar, nursing his bourbon, then slowly sipping from the drink Clemens had left behind. Only when he estimated that his friend had won the three dollars required for the telegram did he step to Clemens's side. "You've made your point, Sam. There's still time to get to the telegraph office before it closes for the evening."

Clemens waved the gambler away. "Not now, Chance. I'm on a roll. A few more games and we'll be eating steak tonight. We can send the wire in the morning." With that, he signaled the next challenger to approach the green-felt field of combat.

"Sam," Chance began again, "we *have* to send that wire before the telegraph office closes—"

"It's too late for that, gentlemen. The office just closed." A man pushed his way through the crowd about the billiard table. "What's all the excitement?"

Chance's stomach twisted into knots, the bourbon now burning like fire. He recognized the man; the last time the gambler had seen him had been in the telegraph office.

"This here stranger has been beatin' every man in town at billiards," one townsman said, and another added, "Even took six bits off Monty Ward in three straight games!"

"Betting?" The telegrapher eyed Clemens, then found Chance before the gambler could sink back and hide himself in the crowd. "Just what did this man use for his side of the wager?"

"A gold pocket watch!" The first man who had fallen to defeat at the writer's hands stepped forward. "A pretty un too!"

"You didn't happen to take a close look at that watch, did you, Charlie Sutton?" When the man shook his head, the telegrapher added, "I didn't think so. 'Cause if you had, you might have noticed that the watch didn't work. This man and his friend over there tried to push that piece of junk off on me over at the office early this afternoon. You've been sold a pig in a poke."

The crowd in the saloon went silent. Every eye in the place turned to Clemens. None of them held love.

As quietly as possible, Chance began to back-step. Men will laugh off being taken in a horse trade and ending up with a one-eyed mare on their hands, or they grin and chuckle when they spend a dollar for a bottle of elixir from a medicine-show man that turns out to be nothing more than a shot of redeye, some sugar, water, and shoe polish. But when it comes to gentlemanly pastimes such as poker or billiards, a matter of honor is involved. Men will just as well kill as look at someone who transgresses that code of honor. It was clear the men of Longway had done all the looking they felt was necessary.

"Pig in a poke!" a nameless voice broke the silence. "It

ain't right he done Charlie like that," another man answered.

"Ain't jest Charlie he hoodwinked. It's all of us," a third man said, which brought a grumble of agreement from the crowd.

"We know how to deal with snakes in Longway, don't we, boys!" yet another of the townsfolk suggested.

If Chance had clung to a hope that he and Clemens might talk their way out of this situation, that hope slipped from his fingers. The moment grown men start calling themselves "boys," as though the old saying "boys will be boys" would somehow account for the less than rational acts of adults, it was time to move on.

Apparently the writer recognized the signs of a brewing storm. He snatched his winnings from the billiard table, pivoted, and ran for the door, but was snared by a jungle of angry arms two strides later. That was one more stride than Chance managed before five men jumped him.

"I'm a mind to geld these two bucks," one of the townsmen proposed.

Another shouted, "Let's stretch their necks a mite!"

Chance doubled his struggle to break free of the arms and hands that held him immobile. Getting hanged for three dollars wasn't the way he envisioned ending his life. Fight as he did, the men of Longway only tightened their hold.

"Boys, boys! It's the likker in your blood a-talkin'. We don't want to kill these two."

Hope sprang anew in Chance's heart when he heard a voice of reason call out from the angry crowd.

"We jest want to teach 'em a lesson they won't forget. I got a bin full of mattress feathers and three buckets of tar over at the store. You're welcome to 'em at half price!"

A roar of approval went up from the men as yet another Longway merchant discovered a method of milking a profit from the misfortunes of others. The crowd surged forward, shoving gambler and writer outside and into the town's muddy main street.

"Fire! Fire!" A young boy ran toward the crowd with his arms waving wildly above his head. "Fire! Fire on the river!"

The men around Chance grew silent as the boy approached.

"It's the sidewheeler *Tuck Finn!* She blowed a boiler and flames are a-lickin' at her decks!" The boy slid to a shaky halt in the mud. Water dripped from the top of the youth's red head to his mud-encased, bare feet. No matter what his real name, Chance was damned glad to see George Peters-Jackson-Elexander. "It's a horrible sight. Men and women screamin' and throwin' themselves in the river!"

"A riverboat burnin?" one man questioned, but before he could continue, another spoke up, having found a way to turn disaster into quick cash. "There'll be salvage enough for the whole town."

"Hold on a minute, Cletus." This from the telegrapher who stepped forward and suspiciously eyed the youth. "Son, I don't reckon I've ever seen you 'round town before."

"No, sir, ya haven't," the water-soaked George Peters-Jackson-Elexander answered. "My name's Butch Smith. I was aboard the *Tuck Finn*. My pap threw me overboard, and I swum for the shore and ran straight here for help. You've got to come. Please, it's horrible!"

So much for his first name being "George," the gambler thought as the boy spewed out yet another alias.

There was no way to stop Longway's men once the scent of salvage wafted to their noses. Throwing Chance and Clemens aside, they sprinted westward toward the river.

"Come on," the boy urged, grinning at his two companions. "Odell's waitin' at the raft. We can be midriver 'fore them folks realize there ain't no sidewheeler a-burnin'."

Neither Clemens nor the gambler questioned the boy's timely rescue. Nor did they pause long enough to thank him for saving them from being fitted for a new suit of tar and feathers. Instead, they ran at his heels and leaped aboard the waiting raft.

George's estimate of their timing proved correct. The raft had just reached midriver when the townsmen of Longway appeared on the bank shouting their curses into the wind. Chance and his companions laughed with relief, none of them minding the drizzle that once more fell from the sky.

SIX

While Chance manned the raft's rudder, Clemens, Odell, and Tuck—the boy now claimed that his name was Tucker Bagg, the son of a mountain man and a Sioux squaw—restoked the fire and fried two hens Odell and Tuck had "found." Cornmeal, also "found," provided a skillet of cornbread to go with the crisp chicken. And for dessert, there were "found" peppermint sticks. The gambler was certain which of the two had "found" these last items.

Tuck, feeling puffed up to about twice his size after the rescue, explained that he and Odell were in Longway reconnoitering the village for useful items that needed "finding" when they heard a ruckus at the saloon. "We went over to take a look and realized ya'll two had stepped into a pile of it."

A watering trough rather than the river had served to drench the boy. While Tuck ran through the town shouting "Fire," Odell returned to the raft to prepare for a quick escape. So proud of the successful rescue was the boy that he rewarded himself with another peppermint stick, his third, before crawling into the tent for a well-earned nap. Clemens smoked half of one of his resurrected cigars before he stretched out atop the logs and quickly drifted into sleep.

Odell relieved the gambler at the rudder and suggested he might consider sleep as well. Consider was all Chance did. For the first time since that original night aboard the raft, the wood refused to accommodate his body. After tossing and turning for an hour, he gave it up. Quietly rising, he eased to the back of the raft and sat beside Odell.

The black spoke of his lost wife and son as they drifted through the Mississippi night. "Boy's eight years now, and he don't even know what his daddy looks like. That ain't right, Duke."

"Chance, Chance Sharpe," the gambler corrected.

"Mr. Chance," Odell said.

"Just Chance."

"Well, Chance," Odell continued, "I intend to correct that. I got plans, ain't nothin' big, but with luck, me and my family'll have a good life. A man can't ask the Lord for more than that."

The gambler nodded in agreement. A good life was what most men searched for, though too often they ran aground on a hidden sandbar.

While Odell spoke of buying a wagon and traveling the Oregon Trail, Chance watched the night. The earlier drizzle had passed, replaced by a muggy night with enough water in the air that fish would have been able to breathe in it. Here and there patches of fog hung over the river, thick and steamy against a man's skin.

It was as the raft slid out of one of these minor clouds come to earth that Odell pointed ahead. "There's somethin' downriver, Chance. Can't make out what it is."

"Steer clear," the gambler said as he pushed to his feet and peered into the darkness. He immediately countermanded himself. "Odell, that's a riverboat. Bring us alongside. She's half sunk, probably lying in a shallow."

Five minutes later, the black man did just that with such skill that the raft edged beside the dying paddlewheeler without so much as a sound to wake Clemens and Tuck. Chance tied the raft's line to a support column that pushed upward from the vessel's half-submerged main deck.

"There," Chance said as he pointed to a wide rent in the sternwheeler's side. "Look, she did run aground on a shallow bar. She's liable to split in two and sink the minute a strong gust of wind comes up."

Odell didn't follow the gambler's hand. Instead, he

nodded upward. "Didn't you and the king say you was aboard a steamer called the *Gulf Runner?*"

"Yes. Why?" Chance glanced up and understood why his companion had asked the question. Even in the dark he could discern the black letters painted on the riverboat's whitewashed texas deck—*Gulf Runner*. "I'll be damned!"

"Not as damned as this steamer is," Odell replied in a low reverent tone. "We should be pushin' on. People's like to have died aboard. Ain't no need to go stirrin' up the dead. Better to let 'em sleep their sleep. Cast off that line."

Chance could only guess what had crippled the stern-wheeler; there were as many things that could kill a riverboat as means for a man to die. However, the one thing he was not going to do was cast off. Whatever misfortune had claimed the *Gulf Runner* was now his fortune.

"Odell, I'm going aboard. I had some money tucked away in a valise in my stateroom when I was thrown overboard," the gambler said. "If I can find that money, there'll be enough to buy passage for all of us on the first riverboat we find heading south."

"Please, Chance, don't do it." Odell shook his head and clutched the mojo bag around his neck. "Ain't no good to come out of walkin' the decks of a ghost boat. Just untie that line, and we'll be on our way."

"This won't take long." The gambler ignored the man's superstition-born doubts, and began to climb the jigsaw work to the riverboat's boiler deck. "I be right back," he whispered down the moment he reached the walkway.

There was good reason for that whisper. Having spent the majority of his life on rivers and riverboats, Chance was well aware that while the *Gulf Runner* appeared abandoned, in all likelihood she wasn't. A dying boat like the steamer offered a ripe prize for plucking. The captain, hoping to waylay losses, probably had left a guard aboard to keep river scavengers away. The salvage value of even a small boat like the *Gulf Runner*, especially if she were carrying cargo, could amount to a small fortune.

It was that guard, ready to give a dose of hot lead to

anyone coming aboard the craft, who sat at the forefront of Chance's mind as he crept around to the opposite side of the boat. He found the window to his stateroom; it opened easily. With a glance to each side to make certain he went undetected, he ducked into the room.

Giving his eyes a few moments to adjust to the interior darkness, the gambler felt his way around the room. His knees smacked into a chair near the bed, providing a sinking feeling in his stomach as well as a shooting pain through his shins. The chair was out of place. So was a nightstand that he stumbled into seconds later.

He tried to tell himself that the stateroom's furniture had been rearranged by members of the *Gulf Runner*'s crew after it was discovered that he was missing from the paddlewheeler. He couldn't quite believe it. A chair might be moved, but it was unlikely that a table would be rearranged so that it stood at the foot of the bed rather than near the headboard.

Of course, he still tried to convince himself, *the furniture might have been tossed around in the accident that befell the* Gulf Runner.

A suitcase stuffed with petticoats and silky underthings open atop the bed, as though someone had attempted to gather her belongings before abandoning the boat, was all he needed to tell him that the captain hadn't hesitated in rebooking the stateroom the moment he had discovered one of his passengers had mysteriously vanished.

With a mumbled curse, Chance sank to the edge of the bed and tried to gather his thoughts. There were two places his property might be stored, below, in the hold, which was now beneath the water and inaccessible, or in the captain's cabin.

Rising, the gambler felt his way to the stateroom's only door, which opened onto the riverboat's main cabin. Cautiously, he twisted the brass doorknob and opened the door a crack. With one eye he peered into the saloon, expecting to find the sentry posted stoically beside the steamer's bar, having himself a sample of the wares left behind when the vessel was abandoned. The gambler saw no one.

Edging the door wider, he slipped into the main cabin. He took a step forward toward the captain's cabin, then abruptly turned back to the stateroom beside his own— Clemens's room. While it was unlikely that his stateroom would have been cleared for new passengers and the writer's left untouched, he couldn't overlook the possibility that his friend's belongings—more important, his money —remained there.

Clemens's stateroom was worse than his own. It was totally bare. Apparently, there had been no rebooking since it was discovered they had vanished from the paddle-wheeler.

Another curse of frustration hissed from his lips when he reentered the saloon. By pressing close to the line of stateroom doors that formed the wall of the cabin, he avoided painful collisions with all but four of the tables and chairs that had been scattered about the long, narrow room when the sternwheeler had gone down.

There was no difficulty in locating the captain's cabin. The pale, yellow glow of a burning tallow candle came from beneath the door. The string of curses that whispered from Chance's lips would have encircled the crippled vessel five times if they had been placed end to end. He had located the guard; the trouble was, the man had decided to station himself exactly where the gambler wanted to be.

The question now was how to get him out of the cabin long enough to search the stateroom.

Returning to his own stateroom and tossing around the furniture would cause enough racket to draw the guard from the captain's cabin. The gambler could then slip out the window, move down the walkway and duck into the window of the captain's room. There were two major snags to that line of attack. First, the man wouldn't remain in the stateroom more than moments after he discovered it was empty. Second, there was no guarantee that the window to the captain's stateroom was open.

Plan two was to return outside and bang a chair against

the wails of the boiler deck until the guard came to investigate. The snag to this approach was more like a sandbar than a snag. The guard would most certainly discover the raft and its occupants moored below.

Then I could always walk up and knock on the door and talk with the guard.

What seemed like a totally ludicrous solution to the problem appeared more viable when examined a second time. The guard would be less inclined to shoot him if he directly approached the man rather than being discovered aboard the boat like some thief hiding in the night. A polite, rational explanation of his plight might, just might, work. The worst that could happen would be that the sentry wouldn't believe his story and would throw him off the *Gulf Runner*. The gambler would be no worse off than he was at the moment.

Actually, Chance realized the guard's reaction might be far worse than that, but he tried not to deflate the sudden surge of courage coursing through him. Drawing a bolstering breath, he crossed the ten feet separating him from the cabin. He lifted his right hand, pausing just before his knuckles rapped the wood.

Voices came from within the room.

Puzzled, the gambler leaned against the door and pressed an ear to the wood. He was right; he heard not one, but two voices, perhaps three, inside the cabin.

This doesn't make sense. Chance edged back. His eyes narrowed, and his lips pursed. The *Gulf Runner* was too small a boat to be carrying cargo valuable enough to warrant three guards. Something was wrong here.

Backing farther away from the cabin, the gambler halted when the doorknob for a stateroom pressed into his back. He turned and opened the door. As quietly as possible, he wove through the furniture scattered across the floor and pulled the window up. Outside he crept along the guard way until he pressed his back flat against the wall beside the half-opened window to the captain's cabin.

"You got it all wrong." There was desperate fear in the

voice of a man that drifted into the night. "I wasn't trying to cross you. I'll swear on a stack of Bibles, if that's what you want. I'd never go against you. You know that. We've been working together too long. A man doesn't turn on his partner."

There was a harsh laugh and the thud of something heavy hitting the wooden floor. "Have him explain this bag then. There's a thousand in hard cash inside and at least twice that much in jewelry."

"It wasn't me!" the first man answered in haste. "You didn't find that sack on me. It was Frank and Steve. They was trying to hold out on you. You know that. It was them that had the sack and was trying to hide it away, not me."

Another cold, humorless chuckle came in reply. The sound sent a shiver up the gambler's spine. The first man's pleas fell on deaf ears.

"Oh, I believe you, Wilt—"

The third voice stiffened every muscle in Chance's body. There was no way he could have mistaken it; Brad Calloway was in that room!

"I know that sack belonged to Frank and Steve. What I want to know is where you stashed your cut of the goods you three were withholding from us."

"Go ahead and slit his throat, Brad. You're wastin' time with this snivelin' pig. We got to go through this bucket room by room anyway. We'll find out where he hid the goods." This came from a fourth man.

Dropping to his belly, the gambler inched beneath the window and cautiously lifted his head until he peeked above the window ledge. Calloway and two of his trained gorillas, Benny and Earl, loomed over a fourth man who sat tied hand, foot, and chest to a chair. The bound man's profile was vaguely familiar. Chance was certain that he was an officer aboard the *Gulf Runner*.

It was more than obvious that the man and Calloway and his companions had been in cahoots, when the officer and two other men had tried to work a double cross. The price that Frank and Steve had paid for their treachery was also obvious; both men were stretched out cold and still on the cabin's floor. Dark pools of blood gathered around their heads, having spilled from the second mouths that were cut in their throats. Chance barely recognized the corpses as Calloway's missing gorillas.

"No! Brad, you can't do that to me. We've known each other too long! We've worked too many jobs together," the officer pled as Calloway pulled a silver-bladed, palm knife from his pocket. "We've been partners for ten years. You can't just up and—"

The palm knife's blade was but three inches long. However, that was more than enough unyielding steel to open the officer's throat from ear to ear in one blurred slash. Blood fountained from the smooth wound and in mere seconds the officer slumped in the chair—dead.

"All in all, not a bad day's work," one of the gorillas laughed. "What started as a sixth each is now a third apiece. It's hard to beat that."

But that was exactly what Calloway was going to do. Chance caught his breath as he watched the blond weasel wipe the palm knife on a handkerchief, and then place cloth and blade back in his pocket. When his hand came out, it held a stubby .32 caliber pistol. The man had no other need for the weapon except to use it to eliminate the remaining two gorillas. All of the ill-gotten gains was better than a mere third cut.

Calloway's face went as hard and as cold as granite when his thumb lifted and gently cocked the revolver's hammer. Slowly, calculating, the man began to turn.

Just then Chance slipped—an elbow jerking away from an insect intent on dining for the night. A hollow wooden thud sounded as the gambler's hand slapped the deck to regain support.

"What the hell was that?" one of the human gorillas questioned in a growl.

"I don't know." This from Calloway. "It came from outside. Benny, check it out."

Chance didn't wait for a head to poke out from the window. Shoving to his feet, the gambler turned and ran aft along the boiler deck. He had overstayed his welcome, and there was no sense waiting around to see how Calloway and his toughs would react to their unexpected guest.

Behind him he heard the sound of a window being thrown open. "Hey! There's someone out here!"

"Get him!" Calloway shouted. "We can't risk any witnesses!"

Which was exactly what the gambler was thinking. He doubled his pace as he rounded the aft portion of the deck. Calloway had already murdered three men this night, a fourth would be of little consequence to him. "Untie the raft! Shove off!"

Chance heard pounding feet on the deck as he vaulted over the boiler deck's rail onto the raft.

"What is it?" Odell asked, his eyes wide as he freed the line.

"It isn't ghosts!" Chance moved beside the rudder and swung the small craft toward the center of the river. The current seemed to move like molasses in the winter, gradually carrying the raft out and away from the crippled steamer. The gambler mentally estimated the distance between him and the riverboat: *Twenty yards, thirty, forty, fifty . . .*

He had reached a hundred when he heard Calloway shout, "There he is! He's getting away."

The next sound that rent the night was the bark of pistols—three of them.

"Down!" Chance shouted, hitting the log deck a split-second behind Odell.

Watery splats came from around the raft as the three men aboard the *Gulf Runner* emptied their guns at the departing craft. Five of the bullets dug into the logs themselves, but all eighteen shots went wild, missing their human marks. By the time Calloway and his gorillas reloaded, the raft had drifted beyond range.

Chance picked himself up and stared back at the riverboat. He heard two more shots ring out, saw the yellow-blue blossoms of flame jump from a single barrel. The last two blasts weren't aimed at the raft. He imagined Benny and Earl crumpling to the deck as Calloway laid claim to all the stolen goods he would strip from the paddlewheeler.

A rumble of thunder came from the west just as three raindrops smacked the gambler in the face. He shivered; somehow another storm just wasn't as important as it had seemed earlier.

SEVEN

The Mississippi did not require the Biblical forty days and forty nights. Three of each—with the sky opening up and rain falling like an impenetrable wall of water—were sufficient to swell the great river until it spilled over its banks and devoured the bottomlands that normally confined the current.

In the first hour of the raging storm that raced up from the Gulf of Mexico, Clemens, Odell, and George if-that-was-his-first-name-and-whatever-his-last-name-might-be had abandoned their colorful descriptions of gully-washer and frog-strangler. By the third they were mumbling—without a hint of jest in their voices—phrases like "the mother of all storms" and "the Good Lord's second flood." The rain, accompanied by a howling wind, spidery legs of lightning that leaped from horizon to horizon, and the constant roll of thunder near and far, provided the gambler with little ammunition to rebut his companions' muttered hyperboles.

With the coming of the fourth hour of riding out the storm on the river, his three companions reached a mutual agreement to abandon their wave-rocked vessel and seek high ground. Chance would have enjoyed taking credit for their sudden insightful display of rational and logical thinking, but he had absolutely no influence on the decision. The pilot at the sticks of a massive sidewheeler blinded by the deluge and doing his damnedest to dodge sandbars and to keep from plowing his bow into the bank, came within a hairbreadth of running smack dab over the raft. Only

62

Odell's quick reaction at the rudder had spared the logs and their occupants a short, sweet, watery end.

Although steamer pilots were well known for delighting in scaring the bejeezus out of men aboard lesser crafts—often actually grazing the hulls of flat- and keelboats alike—this pilot had simply been unable to see the raft and the four men huddled beneath the tent raised on her deck. If one pilot had been unable to make out the raft on the water, odds were pilots at the helms of the other paddlewheelers steaming up and down the Mississippi wouldn't be able to see the craft any better. River Russian roulette was not a game to be taken lightly; the raft was swung to a massive island that thrust up from the rain-pelted water on the Arkansas side of the river.

While Odell, Clemens, and the gambler secured the raft and what meager possessions were aboard, George ran off into the heavy poplar and beech forest that covered the island. He was back in fifteen minutes pointing to a hill at the center of the island. "There's a cave up yonder. Ain't big, but it's fair sized. Should hold the four of us. And most important, it's dry as a bone."

The latter attribute was all that was required to sell the three men he traveled with. Rain ran from their heads to their feet in raging rivulets while they tramped through the wood and slipped and slid their way up the hill.

The cave *was* dry as promised. It was also unoccupied by beast, varmint, or vermin, as added value—although that had not always been the case. Several snake skins, rattlers if Chance was any judge, lay near the east wall of the cave, and a distant aroma hung in the air, barely discernible over the natural musty smell of their temporary shelter, that bespoke of a family of skunks that had used the cave as a residence in the not-too-distant past.

More important was clear evidence that men had once used the cave. A pile of wood stood against the west wall, and a dark circle of ash at the center of the floor marked where a fire had burned. Whether it was hunters, river pirates, or merely adventurous boys come to the island on a lark, it didn't matter. The four thanked their predecessors for the thoughtfulness of leaving the wood, built a fire, stripped away their soaked clothing, hunkered down near the warming flames, and watched the rain fall outside. Nor, as time passed, was the steady rising of the river overlooked.

Observing the storm and the Mississippi weren't the only activities the four had to occupy the sudden overabundance of leisure they found on their hands. Occasionally one of the four had to venture into the forest and gather fresh firewood. This was placed beside the fire, along with wet clothes, to dry.

However, the majority of the time was relegated to lying. To be certain, these all-out, go-for-broke liar contests began innocently enough with Clemens dropping into his Mark Twain persona and recounting the tale of Mr. Smiley and his celebrated jumping frog to help pass the minutes that dragged by like hours. Innocent, though it was, that beginning was enough to start George whatever-his-name-was retelling a never-lived life among the gang of Sam One-Eye Johnson, who along with his fifty cut-throat river pirates, terrorized the Missouri River from Saint Louis to Fort Benton. That Chance had never heard of this bloody murderer didn't stop the boy from detailing his infamous deeds. Odell then joined in with a yarn relating the mysterious, supernatural abilities of Mama Red, who conjured the dead and commanded a full battalion of demons.

So it went from the first moment of waking until their eyes fluttered to sleep each night. Although each tale the three of them uttered was more outrageous than the one that went before, none was able to break the sullen mood that settled over the gambler. He sat quietly watching the sheets of wind-thrown rain pelt the growing freshwater ocean that surrounded their haven of refuge. His mind was elsewhere—on a life that had apparently left him behind, marooned him with fellow castaways who seemed unaware of the predicament they were in. Or if they were, the three of them just didn't seem to care. Worse was Clemens, who relished every moment of this "great adventure."

For Chance the adventure now centered on one pivotal point—how to end it. As much as he hated to admit it, there appeared to be but one method available to him to conclude what was stretching into an unwanted ordeal. He was going to have to go to work!

Whether it meant chopping wood, doing handyman jobs, or shoveling river silt from flooded barns after the Mississippi receded, he would bend his back and apply a bit of old-fashioned elbow grease. It was the only way he would be able to earn the three dollars needed to telegraph New Orleans. He didn't have a stake to sit in on a poker game, and even if he did, no self-respecting gambler would allow him at a table dressed the way he was. Nor did he intend to let Clemens close to another billiards table or cue stick. The possibility of wearing tar and feathers appealed far less to him than continuing to wear the rather shaggy-looking suit he had worn since Calloway and his men tossed him over the side of the *Gulf Runner*.

While the gambler brooded and Clemens, Odell, and George if-that-was-his-name lied to one another, the third night of continual storm gave way the fourth morning to drizzle. This turned to a light mist by noon. The sun actually broke through the clouds when it sat ten degrees above the western horizon.

The bright yellow light was all that was needed for George to proclaim, "It's time we gave this island a fittin' look-see."

Clemens and Odell agreed, grateful for any excuse to get out of the small cave and stretch their legs. Chance waved away the offer to accompany them. Instead, he sat on his heels at the mouth of the cave and stared at the water rushing by below. Here and there broken limbs were whipped downriver by the rushing current. If it wasn't a limb, it was a whole tree uprooted by the summer flood. After counting twenty such trees, the gambler grew bored and scanned the river, searching for more interesting debris to occupy his mind.

That was when he saw the skiff. In the distance, he first thought the small boat to be a wooden crate washed from the deck of a steamboat. But a quarter of a mile from the island, its shape and form were unmistakable: it was a skiff! And it was being washed directly toward the island.

In truth, he admitted, it wasn't much of a boat. Perhaps rowboat would have more aptly described the small craft, since it would have been difficult to get four grown men into it and still keep it afloat. But riding in the skiff hadn't entered Chance's mind. What he saw rushing head-on atop the Mississippi were dollar bills!

He tried to contain his excitement, but with little success. The pounding in his temples was hard to ignore. If the boat continued on its present course, it would be washed into the island. All he had to do was walk to the water's edge, secure it, then sell the craft at the next town they happened upon. In spite of its smallness, the boat would bring at least five dollars.

If it's in decent condition. Chance once more attempted to waylay the adrenaline now coursing through his veins.

There was no way to quell the race of his pulse. A small whirlpool an eighth of a mile from the bank caught the skiff's prow, acted like a slingshot, and hurled the boat directly to the bank.

Chance shoved from his haunches and raced down the hill. Weaving through poplar and beech and ducking low-slung branches, he reached the water's edge just as the skiff touched the shore and started to drift out into the river again. The gambler snaked out an arm and snared a rope tied to the small craft's bow. After tying the rope around the trunk of a sapling, he hauled the boat back to the bank.

A frown of unwanted surprise creased Chance's brow. The skiff wasn't empty. A man lay stretched out facedown in the bottom of the boat. He didn't move—not even to breathe.

The gambler held no doubts as to the fact that the man

was dead when he carefully stepped into the skiff and knelt beside the body. The boat slid out to the limits of the twenty-foot rope, but Chance didn't notice or care. He was too busy rolling the death-stiffened corpse to its back.

He had read descriptions in novels that placed grimaces of pain or horror on the faces of the dead. He had always discounted such as poetic license, because every expression he had ever viewed on a dead man was the same— eyes wide and face blank. Muscles that relaxed as life fled them left features flaccid. This man's face was no different —except for a single dark hole that opened in the center of his forehead. One pistol shot had claimed the man's life.

Chance expected the water gathered in the bottom of the skiff to be tinted red with the dead man's blood, but it wasn't. That meant the man had died elsewhere and his body had been placed in the boat. Whether the skiff had been set adrift or had escaped the man's murderers in the storm was a matter of conjecture that would probably never have an answer.

Lifeless and cold, it was difficult to estimate the man's age from his face. But the gambler placed him and his salt-and-pepper hair in his early fifties. The suit he wore was simple black, cut from even simpler cloth; it gave no hint as to the man's profession or station in life. He might have been a farmer in his sole Sunday-go-to-meeting attire or a businessman traveling the river until foul play abruptly ended his travels.

The gambler slipped a hand into the right pocket of the black coat. He came up empty-handed, except for several bits of soggy tobacco that clung to his fingertips. *A pipe smoker,* Chance guessed, although he found no pipe in either the right or left pockets.

Laying open the man's coat, he slipped a leather wallet from the coat's interior pocket. He caught his breath when he opened the billfold and found five ten-dollar bills staring back at him!

Mere moments ago he had mentally celebrated peddling this skiff for five dollars. Now he held fifty dollars in his hands—more than enough to wire New Orleans!

Yet, Chance could not bring himself to pull the bills from the wallet. He had watched soldiers strip the dead on the battlefield—Union and Rebel alike. The sight had churned his stomach. To take the fifty—even one of the tens—smacked too closely of the horrors of war he had witnessed. There had to be another way.

Sucking down a deep breath, the gambler realized that there was. It would be more complicated and take longer, but it didn't involve robbing the dead. He would do exactly as he had planned. He would take the skiff—and the body —to the next town downriver and turn the corpse over to the proper authorities. Sheriff, constable, chief of police, it didn't matter which, there would be the inevitable questions as to who he was and how he happened to stumble upon a dead man with a bullet hole in the center of his skull. To verify his answers, they would have to telegraph New Orleans, and that meant contact with his attorney.

Although Chance didn't relish an encounter with the police in any form—lawmen, especially along the river, frowned on those who made a living via cards, dice, and the roulette wheel—his plan was preferable to looting a dead man. Pleased with his decision, the gambler started to close the wallet when two pieces of white paper in another of the billfold's compartments caught his eye.

Careful not to rip the soggy paper, he gently eased the paper from the leather. Both were letters; the addresses were smeared and ink ran across the pages in splotchy blots. The first letter was totally indecipherable. However, the second appeared—if the gambler read the running ink correctly—to be addressed to a John M. Seese. Chance couldn't make out the city, but Seese was apparently from the state of New York. The return address on both letters had been obliterated by the water.

Chance patted the water-soaked letters back inside the wallet and closed it. He then returned letters and money to the pocket from which he had taken them. He would have to get Mr. Seese's body to the authorities quickly. With the cooling rains of the storm past, the summer sun and its heat would soon begin to work on the corpse. It was time to return his three companions to the raft and head downriver again.

Standing, he noticed for the first time that the rushing floodwaters had pulled the skiff away from the bank so that it strained at the end of its mooring line. Chance leaned forward to grab the rope and haul himself back to the shore.

That was the way the log caught him—stooped over and off balance. The flood-driven battering ram slammed solidly into the side of the small rowboat, jarring the craft in a wobbly dance as it rode the water.

Fight to right himself as he did, the gambler could not regain his balance. With curses bursting form his lips, Chance swayed on the side of one foot for an instant before toppling into the river.

The current gripped the gambler the moment his body was immersed in the water. Like a liquid hand, it wrapped around his torso, arms, and legs, pulling him outward.

The gambler's head came out of the water with a toss to the side to clear the moisture from his eyes. The chilling cold deepened. In no more than a second or two, the current had swept him twenty feet from the skiff. His arms stretched out and his legs kicked. For five minutes, he swam toward the island, only to discover that he now bobbed a hundred yards from the bank. Even as he checked his position, the floodwaters sucked him farther and farther from the warm, dry shelter of the cave, and his three friends who wandered somewhere in the woods.

EIGHT

The branch wasn't large enough to sit atop, but did support Chance's weight when he draped both arms around it and clung to it for his life. Which is exactly what he did while the sun disappeared in the west and a half-moon poked in and out of the drifting clouds overhead.

An outstretched hand with fingers splayed wide represents fifteen arc degrees from thumb to little finger when held against the sky. That was roughly the distance the stars, planets, and moon move in an hour period. It was thus that the gambler estimated his time in the river.

Four hours passed before a boiling sink caught the limb, submerged it and the man clinging to it and threw them back to the surface. Other than almost filling his lungs with water and drowning him, the incident would have been meaningless except for the fact that the gambler noticed a slight change in the current that swept him downriver. No longer was he pulled toward the center of the Mississippi, but instead, once more drifted toward the Arkansas bank.

The moon settled behind the horizon, and Chance selected a bright star in the constellation of Aquila, the Eagle, as a yardstick to measure the passage of time. Two hours crept by before he could separate the dark silhouettes on the shore into the shapes of individual trees. As best he could judge, a quarter of a mile stood between him and dry land.

Without a second thought to what he did, the gambler released his hold on the limb and kicked for the bank.

A quarter of a mile might as well have been a hundred

70

miles. The force of the rushing floodwaters had not diminished. Although his long, striving strokes brought him closer, it was usually only by a matter of inches. And those were lost backwards whenever he paused to estimate the progress he made as the water tugged him.

It was while he treaded water trying to judge the distance to shore that he hit another sink!

Without the tree limb for buoyancy, he was sucked down by the turbulent water. Helplessly, he spun head over heels beneath the water, tossed unmercifully by the current. He fought with arms and legs to break free of the sweeping water, but his actions brought no results. The maelstrom of water made it impossible to tell up from down; he didn't know whether the water still sucked him toward the river's muddy bottom or thrust him toward the surface.

Nor did remaining motionless and letting his natural buoyancy carry him upward work. The chaos of the sink was indecipherable. All he could was hold his breath and silently pray.

The burning in the gambler's lungs began far too soon, it seemed. An aching sensation deep in his chest pushed outward, demanding the air his body so desperately needed. Still Chance held out, clamping a hand over nose and mouth to stop the irrepressible desire to breathe, for he would be breathing water.

Seconds that seemed like hours dragged on, and still the current somersaulted him beneath the water. Then without the slightest hint of warning, his head broke the surface. His mouth jerked wide, and he sucked down cool air into his fiery lungs. Three more deep gulps to quiet the ache in his chest, and he splashed around to regain his bearings.

Tree limbs drifted overhead. Or as the case was, he rushed beneath them. The sink had tossed him mere feet from the bank!

Stretching out an arm, Chance snagged the first branch his fingers touched. It snapped beneath his weight, as did the second and third branches he caught. However, the fourth held. He reached up with his left arm, and held on with both hands. After several long moments to ascertain whether this limb would support him, he began drawing himself hand-over-hand toward the shore.

There was a solidness to mud that he had never perceived before when his feet squished atop the bank. Slipping and sliding, he worked up the slight incline, until grass replaced mud beneath his boots, then he dropped to the ground and rolled to his back. Closing his eyes, he drew a grateful breath and sighed with relief. Exhaustion overcame him almost immediately, and he dropped into sleep.

A cool summer morning breeze carrying the scent of daisies bathed Chance's face. Without opening his eyes to push back the gentle sleep, he smiled. The fragrance was reminiscent of perfume, something he had not smelled in more days than he wanted to remember.

Rolling over in the soft bed, he nestled his face against the pillow, enjoying the freshness of the linens—

Bed? Awareness sliced through the sleep cotton-clogging his brain. He hadn't slept in a bed since Brad Calloway had unceremoniously dumped him over the side of the *Gulf Runner*. And unless he had totally lost his mind, he had fallen asleep atop a damp riverbank.

The gambler's eyes opened. He *was* in a bed! Linen sheets, carrying the scent of soap and sun-drying, were neatly tucked under his chin. The morning breeze came from an open window hung with white, gauzy curtains that gently stirred with the breath of fresh air. Outside he saw the cultivated fields of a farm. Forest stood beyond the harrowed rows.

Without twitching a muscle in his body, Chance's eyes darted about. He was in a bedroom. And if he was any judge of decor, this bedroom belonged to a woman. The white, ruffled canopy above the bed was a dead giveaway.

How? He didn't have the foggiest memory of ever rising

from the riverbank, let alone somehow managing to talk his way into a woman's bedroom.

To top that off—he was naked! The sweet-smelling sheets around him touched bare flesh, not the rumpled and soiled suit he had been wearing for nearly two weeks. *How?*

Uncertain whether he had lost his mind or was still dreaming, Chance cautiously rolled to his opposite side. "I'm still dreaming" came as a mumble when his eyes met the gaze of three beautiful women who stood beside the bed staring down at him! All were dressed in men's work clothing more suited to the fields outside than the feminine frill of the bedroom.

"Good morning." The woman at the center stepped forward, brushing a stray strand of nut brown hair from her forehead. Her voice betrayed a strong Southern accent, which led the gambler to believe that he might still be in Arkansas, although he wouldn't have been willing to bet on it. A smile uplifted the corners of the young woman's mouth. "My sisters and I were afraid you were going to sleep the whole day away."

"You don't happen to have a name, do you?" This from the young woman on the left. "We never had a guest in our house before without our knowing his name."

"Chance, Chance Sharpe," the gambler muttered as he rolled to his back and closed his eyes. There was no way around it; he was still dreaming, and he was afraid if he questioned these lovely visions, they would evaporate and leave him still lying atop that damp riverbank.

NINE

"Chance Sharpe?" The gambler wasn't certain which of the three women spoke; he still had his eyes closed. "That's a mighty unusual name."

"I was hoping his name would be Odysseus the way we found him cast upon the shore and all," another of the women answered.

"Odysseus was Greek, Marybeth," the first voice replied. "It's plain to see he isn't Greek; he speaks English."

There were two amused giggles and a reprimanding "shhhhh." The latter diminished the giggles, but did not silence them.

The literary reference surprised the gambler. There was a long-standing joke among Texans that proclaimed that settlers reaching the Red River came upon a sign with arrows pointing the way to Texas and Arkansas. Those who could read always took the route to Texas while the remainder ended up in Arkansas. His travels in Arkansas had often proved the claims of illiteracy true. Although, he admitted, the same could be said of the Lone Star State.

Chance opened his eyes again. The three women remained, as did the bedroom and the soft bed beneath his naked body. He still wasn't sure whether he dreamed, but he resisted the urge to pinch himself. Dream or not, the three young women were quite lovely, even beautiful—he was certain that nearly two weeks without laying an eye on a female did nothing to impair his judgment of feminine pulchritude. He drew a deep breath—noting that the floral scent he earlier had attributed to daisies was indeed perfume—and smiled at the trio of ladies.

The one at the center still stood closest to the bed; the other two remained a step behind with hands raised to their mouths to hide their giggles.

"Our family name is Ragglin, Mr. Sharpe." Chance estimated the age of the woman at the center to be no more than twenty-five. Besides soft, nut brown hair that cascaded all the way to her waist, she possessed wide, alluring brown eyes that any red-blooded American male would have given an arm or a leg to view in the moonlight—without a chaperon. "My given name is Caitlyn."

"Caitlyn Ragglin, I'm honored to meet you." A tilt of his head was the best bow the gambler could manage while stretched out flat on his back.

The two younger women, whom Chance estimated to be in their late teens, stifled another giggle behind their hands. Both were as attractive as their older sister, with hair a shade or two lighter than Caitlyn's. What they lacked was the feminine maturity visible in their older sister's eyes. Both were little more than girls—although quite fetching girls.

"This is Lizabeth, Lizzy," Caitlyn continued and the young woman to her right stepped forward. The girl to the left joined her sisters when Caitlyn added, "And this is Marybeth."

Nineteen or twenty, Chance guessed at Lizzy's age, while he placed Marybeth's years at no more than eighteen.

"Is it possible to speak with one of your parents?" he asked. "I'd like to ask them a few questions about the circumstances surrounding my arrival in this household."

Caitlyn visibly stiffened at the mention of her parents. A shadow of a frown darkened her lovely features. "You're talking to the whole Ragglin family at the moment, Mr. Sharpe. Both our mother and father have passed on."

"I'm sorry," Chance mumbled awkwardly. Finding three beautiful young women living alone was totally unexpected. Apparently the eligible men in this portion of Arkansas were all possessed of a serious ailment that affected their eyesight.

"You've no need to be sorry. The Good Lord was gentle when he took both of them," Caitlyn said. Her head gave a little nod to the gambler. "As to how you got in this house and that bed, my sisters and I brought you here. We found you down by the river yesterday morning when we went out to plow the fields."

"Yesterday morning?" Chance's eyes widened, then narrowed at the pronouncement. "You mean I've been out for over a day?"

"Sleeping like a baby." This from Marybeth, who batted long eyelashes over her green eyes.

Lizzy added, "We were afraid you were sick or something when you slept so hard. But as anyone can see, you're quite healthy." Her eyelashes fluttered over hazel eyes with a hue somewhere between brown and green.

"And you brought me here?" The gambler glanced down at himself.

"There are three of us," Caitlyn answered. "We're used to lugging heavy things around the farm. We cleaned the mud off you, and tucked you away here."

Chance could well imagine the series of giggles the act of cleaning the mud off him must have elicited from Marybeth and Lizzy. It was more than obvious that the three sisters hadn't just dunked him in a tub before depositing him in the bed.

Apparently Caitlyn realized the thoughts moving through his head. "There's no need to go getting embarrassed, Mr. Sharpe. We all have seen men in the buff before. Before the war, we had two brothers. After our mother died, we were the ones who nursed them when they got sick."

"Besides, Caitlyn is a widow woman"—a dreamy expression clouded Lizzy's face as she looked at her older sister—"almost, that is. She had a beau who died in Memphis during the war. They were engaged to be married."

Caitlyn shot a stern glance at her sister. "We've both-ered Mr. Sharpe long enough. I'm sure he'll be wanting to rise and eat some breakfast—"

"Chance," the gambler corrected. "Please call me Chance."

"It's time you two were out to the fields," Caitlyn con-tinued. "After all, you were only going to look in on Mr. Sharpe, if you remember rightly."

"Chance," he repeated. "Please call me Chance."

"And who is going to cook Mr.—Chance's breakfast?" Lizzy challenged. "You, Caitlyn?"

"As the oldest, it is my duty to see that guests are re-ceived with our full hospitality," the older sister replied.

Her answer drew a huffy "humph!" from both Lizzy and Marybeth. The younger women's lower lips extended in a slight pout.

"Now, that will be enough from the both of you." Cait-lyn scolded more like a mother than a sister. "You're late for your chores. The corn needs planting, and the potatoes needed to be weeded last week."

With her arms spread wide Caitlyn shooed the two to-ward the bedroom door. "I'll be out to join you as soon as I've seen to Mr. Sharpe's breakfast."

"Chance," the gambler tried again.

"I don't know why you work us so hard, Caitlyn." Marybeth balked at the threshold. "All the plowing and planting isn't going to make any difference, and you know as well as Lizzy and I do."

"She's right, Caitlyn," Lizzy began, but her older sister cut her short.

"I don't want to hear that from either of you!" Anger tinged the older Ragglin sister's tone. "Everything is going to be all right, just like I promised. This land belonged to our daddy, and now it belongs to the three of us. He worked the land and made a good living. We can do the same—we *will* do the same. Do you two understand?"

"But, Caitlyn, what about Uncle—"

"I don't want to hear it. There aren't any buts when it

comes to this farm." Caitlyn edged her sisters from the bedroom. "Now, get outside and go about your chores."

The older sister stood at the doorway watching the two younger women retreat. When she heard a door open and close, she turned back to Chance. The anger that had been in her voice and expression were no longer visible. "If you'll wait here just a moment, Mr. Sharpe—"

"Chance," he implored.

"Chance," she said, conceding. "I'll bring you some clothes."

"I'm not going anywhere," the gambler said as Caitlyn disappeared from the room.

She returned after less than a minute, carrying a neatly folded, starched, white shirt, and a pair of black breeches. She placed the clothing atop a chair. On the floor beside that chair stood Chance's boots—mirror-polished.

"We washed your clothes, but they aren't quite dry yet. The air's been awful damp what with all the rain we've had," Caitlyn said. "These belonged to Father. He was a tall man like yourself—a full six feet. I think they will fit you. When you dress, come downstairs to the kitchen. I'll have a breakfast cooking for you."

The young woman turned to the door, and Chance swung his legs over the side of the bed and sat up. He barely had time to cover himself with a corner of the sheet when Caitlyn reached the doorway and glanced back over a shoulder.

"There's a razor, strap, soap mug, and water atop that table in the corner, should the urge to shave strike you." Her brown eyes moved over his bare chest and legs before she once more turned and walked from the bedroom.

The gambler waited a second or two, to make certain he heard her footsteps retreating down the hall before he slipped from the bed and stretched. The borrowed clothes didn't include underwear, but did have a pair of clean socks. All smelled of cedar; he didn't mind. The odor was clean when compared to the stink of the river.

The razor, soap, and water were where Caitlyn promised. A glance at himself in the mirror above the table was all he needed to understand why the young woman had mentioned a shave. The last time he had grown a forest this thick on his face was in the winter while he wandered through the Dakota Territory. After thoroughly wetting the dense beard, he worked up a lather in the mug and brushed the soap over his cheeks, chin, and neck. The razor felt sharp to his thumb, but he gave it several passes on the leather strap for good measure. By the time it had sawed its way through the beard, it would be a damned sight duller.

Ten minutes later the gambler washed the last traces of soap from his face and ran a hand over now smooth cheeks. He smiled at himself in the mirror. He had forgotten how good a clean-shaven face made a man feel.

In spite of their scent of cedar, the clean shirt and trousers felt fresh against his skin. He slipped on the socks and tugged on his boots. He didn't need direction to find his way downstairs to the kitchen. The aroma of brewing coffee and frying bacon pulled him like iron to a magnet.

Caitlyn smiled when he entered the room, waved an arm to a table covered with a blue-and-white-checkered cloth, and poured a cup of coffee that she set before him. "You don't look like the man we hauled off the riverbank, Mr—Chance. You're a lot younger-looking without all those whiskers. You should consider shaving more often. Some would say you're a handsome man."

"Circumstances beyond my control separated me from my own razor about two weeks ago." The gambler laughed, surprised by the woman's forward approach. He didn't ask if she were among the "some" she had mentioned. Instead, he sipped from the cup. The coffee warmed his throat and empty stomach. "You don't realize just how good this tastes or how fantastic that bacon smells."

Caitlyn forked six strips of crisp-fried bacon from a skillet and placed them on a plate. "I've biscuits cooking and I'd planned to fry you up three eggs, but you can start on this if you've a mind."

"I'd be grateful to start with that bacon." His mouth was watering like an alley mongrel who had sighted a fresh side of beef. That first strip of bacon tasted every bit as good as it smelled. So did the second and third; the remaining pieces he saved until Caitlyn placed the biscuits and eggs on his plate.

"If I'm not prying, what were the circumstances that separated you from your razor?" She took a chair across the table from him and sipped from her own cup of coffee.

"A blond weasel who didn't like losing at poker," Chance answered. Between bites of egg, buttered biscuit, and bacon, he briefly explained his run-in with Brad Calloway and his four gorillas. "My friend and I were pulled from the river by a man and boy on a raft. We've been traveling with them ever since, living off what fish we could catch and berries we foraged in the woods."

He didn't mention the occasional fried chicken George and Odell managed to "find." There was no reason to make this young woman any more suspicious of his moral character than she already must be.

"And your friend and this man and boy, where are they now?" she asked as she poured him another cup of coffee.

Chance gave her an abbreviated version of their time on the island and his finding of the skiff which led to his separation. Like the chickens, he neglected to mention the dead man he had found in the skiff. Again there was no need to aroused unwanted suspicions. "I'd been in the river most of the night when I finally made it to the bank and passed out. I guess that I was more exhausted than I realized to have slept through a whole day."

"I'd say that you are a lucky man, Chance," Caitlyn said when he concluded. "You could have easily drowned in the flood waters. Two men from town did last spring when they were trying to salvage crates from a riverboat out of the river. The Mississippi can be treacherous."

"Not as treacherous as men," he replied.

A distant look covered Caitlyn's face for a moment as she sat poised with her coffee cup in both hands. The gambler could only guess what thoughts took her from the table, or if something he had said had wakened some memory. With a little shake of her head she returned and smiled. "I understand your situation, Chance, and while three dollars isn't much to most people, it's a small fortune to my sisters and myself. I'd loan it to you for that telegram, if I had it."

"I wasn't asking for a loan," Chance said. "I hope you don't think that I was implying such—"

She shook her head, rose from the table, and looked from a window to the farm's fields. "I guess money's been on my mind more than normal since my father died two months ago."

Chance wasn't certain what to say, so he sat there without speaking a word. If this woman wanted to say more, she would in her own time and way.

She did, while she remained at the window: "My father was never a rich man, but he did well by his family with this farm. He raised five children and keep a roof over their heads and food in their mouths. While the clothes we wore might not have been the style of Saint Louis or New Orleans, they kept us warm in the winter and our shoes always had good soles on them."

She paused as though lost in memories for several silent moments. She ran a hand over her head when she spoke again. "When Pa died, he left a will that gave this farm and a few hundred dollars he had saved in the bank to my sisters and me. This land belong to his grandfather, and Pa intended to keep it in the family after he passed on."

"A wise man," the gambler said. "You and your sisters seem to be carrying out his wishes. From what I've seen of the farm from the bedroom window, you're handling yourself well."

"Thank you." She smiled as she returned to her chair across the table from him. "Lizzy, Marybeth, and I helped Pa with all the chores after our brothers went off to war. All of us can handle ourselves as good as any man."

"But?" Chance asked, remembering Marybeth saying

that what they did in the fields would make no difference.

A sad little smile touched Caitlyn's lips. She drew a weighty breath and sighed. "That 'but' is our Uncle John, Pa's half brother. Pa made him our trustee until I turn twenty-five, which is still nine months away. Living way up in New York City and being a banker and all, Uncle John doesn't understand what it is to work Arkansas dirt. He's only given us ten dollars since Pa died, saying it was better to keep the eight hundred in the bank where it would grow with interest. He wrote that he would see to all our needs when he visited us this summer."

Caitlyn paused again and that distant look returned to her face. She sipped at her coffee, but Chance could tell she didn't taste it.

"It really wasn't such a hardship on us, not having spending money," Caitlyn began again. "There had been plenty of times when Pa had been short on cash, so we were used to it. We had all the food we needed, and we could trade eggs and milk for sugar and flour at the general store in Ben Daniel."

"Ben Daniel?" Chance asked.

"It's the nearest town," she replied. "It's seven miles south as the river flows."

The gambler thought he knew most of the towns along the river, but he couldn't recall ever hearing of Ben Daniel. However, if it was large enough to have a bank, he was certain he could find enough odd jobs to earn the three dollars he needed for the telegram.

Caitlyn's voice drew the gambler from his own thoughts: "Two days ago Uncle John suddenly appeared on our doorstep. Mr. Jason Briggs was standing at his side. Mr. Briggs is the president of the Ben Daniel National Bank and Trust."

Caitlyn explained that she had never seen her father's half brother before, but that he carried several letters that she had written to him after her father's death. "He also had all the papers Mr. Briggs had sent him making him executor of the will and our trustee.

"Uncle John and Mr. Briggs spent an hour or two walking around the farm and whispering to each other," Caitlyn continued. "Then they came back to the house and called all three of us into the parlor."

When Caitlyn paused this time, it was because of the tears that welled in her eyes. It took several deep breaths before she steadied herself enough to speak again. "That's when Uncle John announced that three young women had no business trying to run a farm without a man. He said that he had arranged with Mr. Briggs to have the farm put up for public auction and that once it was sold he intended to return to New York City with us and see that we became young ladies as he was sure his brother would have wanted, rather than digging in the dirt like lowborn farmhands."

If the young woman's voice had quavered when she started, Chance heard the anger he had detected earlier when she finished these last words. Gone too were the tears that had misted her eyes. Now they seemed to flare with indignation.

"A lot he knows about what Pa wanted," she said. "We tried to explain that Pa wanted us to keep this land for the husbands and families we would all have one day, but he wouldn't listen." Again she rose and returned to the window to stare out at the fields. "What does a banker from New York City know about a farm like this? He wouldn't even stay in this house with us. He's renting himself a room in a boardinghouse in Ben Daniel. Uncle John hasn't the slightest notion what this farm meant to Pa or what it means to the three of us. He won't even talk with us about keeping the farm."

"When is the auction?" Chance asked.

"Saturday, two days from now," she answered. "So you can see why I can't offer you the money for that telegram."

"Like I said, I wasn't asking for a loan." Chance eased from the table and looked down at his cleaned plate. "However, I can offer to pay for this excellent breakfast, if you don't mind trading a little work for the food."

Caitlyn didn't even suggest that his offer wasn't necessary. Instead, she walked to the door, opened it, and pointed to a woodpile outside. "There's an ax in that old stump."

The gambler nodded and walked outside.

TEN

Chance had never intended to stay on the Ragglin farm longer than was required for the pile of split wood to grow high enough to equal the cost of Caitlyn's excellent breakfast, or until his own clothing dried—whichever came first. However, circumstances, especially when woven around three lovely, young, defenseless women, have a way of taking a man unaware and tangling him up before he notices. All of which left him to ponder who was really the defenseless one.

Halfway through a cord of wood, which the gambler deemed an ample display of sweat to wipe the slate clean for the breakfast and bed (he discounted the bath, since Lizzy and Marybeth's earlier giggles said that they had probably enjoyed it as much as he would have, had he been conscious), a plow harness snapped on Caitlyn. The two mules she worked decided, as was the habit of mules, to make a break for it—in different directions. While Lizzy and Marybeth took a northern course after one of the braying fugitives, he and Caitlyn headed south to track down the other escapee.

A half hour later the wayward animals were apprehended and returned to indenture. They would have been immediately sentenced to hard labor in the fields for their transgressions except for the fact that the harness remained broken. Chance called for an awl and some leather thongs, which Lizzy brought from the barn. Using a pattern like the five-spot on a die, the gambler punched matching holes in the two pieces of the snapped strap, laid them atop each other, then pushed the thongs through the holes to securely bind the broken leather.

By the time the harness was resurrected, Marybeth came trotting from the farmhouse with a lunch bucket brimming with biscuits, fried ham, and hard-boiled eggs in one hand and a jug of morning milk in the other. Chance thoroughly enjoyed the repast with the three sisters, taken atop a blanket spread beneath the shade of a towering oak. However, the second meal of the day also left him with another unpaid obligation.

This he erased by helping Marybeth shovel dried corn into burlap bags, and then loading the sacks onto the bed of a wagon. The corn would be taken into Ben Daniel to be sold or traded, the youngest Ragglin sister explained.

With the public auction of the farm so near, the gambler wondered if the sisters would reap the rewards of this day's labors. However, he didn't openly question the futility of their back-aching work. He had already witnessed Caitlyn's anger when Lizzy and Marybeth had done so that morning. He had no desire to incur the woman's ire.

Corn bagged and neatly stacked in the wagon, Chance was ready to claim his clothing and begin the walk to Ben Daniel and start earning the three dollars needed for his telegram to New Orleans. It was then that Lizzy called out for assistance with a split-rail fence she was mending. The gambler eyed the task and decided he could spare another hour to help the middle sister.

Chance proved to be no better a construction boss than those in the service of governments throughout the country; he underestimated the time to complete the job. When the last of the split logs was raised and the collapsed fence once more stood erect, early afternoon had become late afternoon.

Caitlyn rang the dinner bell.

The red beans and rice, containing less of a hot, spicy bite than the Cajun-style the gambler was accustomed to, left him with a touch of longing for his adopted home of New Orleans. Although he didn't like facing it, the way things were going, it appeared that he would be well into middle age with silver streaking his hair before he walked the narrow streets of the French Quarter again.

The supper conversation revolved around the planting and the growing of crops. Chance had little to contribute, but he enjoyed sitting and listening to the three sisters' voices. After the days in the cave with Clemens, Odell, and George whatever-in-the-world-his-name-was and their all-out liars contest, simple talk about peas, beans, and potatoes somehow sounded like a congregation of the world's intellectuals discussing global problems and possible solutions.

When hot peach pie and coffee were served, Marybeth let slip a reference to the sisters' Uncle John and immediately drew a harsh gaze from Caitlyn. Apparently the man and his future for the farm were strictly taboo with the oldest sister. If that was the way she wanted it, Chance was willing to accept the conditions, although he couldn't see how it would help in finding a solution to the Ragglin sisters' dilemma.

While the gambler worked on a second helping of the pie, Caitlyn excused herself from the table and returned minutes later carrying two blankets and a pillow in her arms. "Chance, you're welcome to stay the night here, if you're of a mind."

The gambler accepted the bedding, realizing that his second night's stay on the Ragglin farm wasn't to be in the soft, clean bed where he had spent the first night.

"Of course," Caitlyn said, "you'll have to make do in the barn. Bringing an unconscious man whom we all thought was dying into the house is one thi g, but allowing a healthy, strong man to stay under the roof with three women is another."

Her voice trailed off in modest embarrassment, which left Lizzy and Marybeth with hands covering their mouths —whether to hide shock or muffled giggles, Chance wasn't sure. The gambler nodded his understanding of the young women's compromising position, wolfed down the last two bites of the peach pie, bid the sisters a pleasant night, then headed for the barn.

An empty stall, in which he spread blankets atop a pile of fresh straw, served nicely as a bed. He didn't even mind the warm aroma of cow and mule manure that hung in the air. In comparison to the street odors of some cities he had been in, it was a clean smell.

The only problem with the sleeping arrangements stemmed from himself, not the barn. In spite of a full day of hard work, he wasn't tired. Stretching out atop the blankets didn't help. Closing his eyes and ordering himself to sleep seemed only to double his wakefulness.

It was the red beans and rice, he decided, that kept back sleep—not that they caused heartburn; rather, they had awakened an intense yearning for New Orleans. Most of all, he missed walking the decks of his own sidewheeler, the *Wild Card*. Just how much, he hadn't realized until this moment.

Old age is creeping up on you, he told himself as he stood. *You're becoming set in your ways.*

The revelation was surprising. When he had won the riverboat in a card game nearly two years ago, he had wanted neither it nor the responsibility inherent in running a paddlewheeler. After receiving the title to the boat, his only thought had been to place the *Wild Card* up for public auction and collect what he could for the luxury steamer.

Two years of fighting and struggling to keep the boat afloat had changed that. He found to his surprise that he liked being a man of property. Enjoyed strolling the *Wild Card*'s decks knowing that they belonged to him. And— his mind stumbled as the thought occurred to him—he liked the financial security that operating a riverboat brought. The gambler's life he had led since age fifteen had been one of feast or famine. The profits the *Wild Card* brought in eliminated those times when he walked around with empty pockets.

The present excluded, he corrected himself.

There was one other thing the *Wild Card* had brought

him that he now admitted he enjoyed—respectability. No matter how the cards were dealt, a gambler was a rogue in the eyes of this country. On the other hand, the proprietor of a riverboat was a man of substance. The *Wild Card* opened doors, admitting him into circles of society that had once paid him no more than a disdaining glance. That, in turn, allowed him to ply his real trade for a more sizable profit—for after all was said, Chance Sharpe remained a gambler first and last.

Reaching the barn's door, Chance gazed over the farm's fields. He estimated the hour to be at least eight in the evening, but the summer sun still had half an hour before it would sink below the horizon. Dusk would linger an hour after that. With sleep evading him, he decided to walk.

There was no design to his strides. He strolled casually, idly. His thoughts remained centered on the *Wild Card*, wondering how long the workmen rebuilding her cannon-shattered decks would labor before she once more steamed up and down the Mississippi and Missouri.

And when she did, would it be the same as it had been before the river pirates' attack with the gunboat? Without a boat beneath their feet for six months, the paddlewheeler's crew had each gone their own way to find employment on other steamers. Chance couldn't blame them. Men and women needed to eat, needed a steady paycheck. And there was no possible way Chance could have paid their salaries for six months without a riverboat to bring in cash.

The *Wild Card*'s young, roguish pilot Henri Tuojacque had been first to find a berth aboard another sidewheeler. He had told the gambler that he had taken the position under the condition that he would return to the *Wild Card* once she was ready to sail again. Pilot Ted Stower had been next to leave. With him had gone apprentice Gary Eakin. Behind them had gone the boats officers, stewards, maids, and roustabouts.

Even Katie MacArt, the *Wild Card*'s fiery redheaded bartender, had returned to her former profession as a waitress aboard another luxury steamer. However, Katie would be back; of that Chance was certain. Owning a liquor concession aboard a riverboat, as she did, was a gold mine no sane person would willingly abandon.

Of all the *Wild Card*'s crew, only the crusty captain Bert Rooker had been retained for the duration of the repairs. Bert now oversaw the reconstruction of the paddlewheeler, making certain the workmen returned the sidewheeler to her former glory.

The gambler paused and glanced around. His unguided footsteps had brought him to the river. A wan smile moved across his lips; he always returned to the river. Other than his father's farm in Kentucky, the rivers of this country were the only home he had ever known or would probably ever know.

The Mississippi's floodwaters had receded twenty feet in the two days since he had floundered to the bank more drowned than alive. The current appeared tame now, compared to the raging torrent he had watched from the shelter of the island cave. But the calmness was a deception, he realized. Until the river returned to its normal channel, the rushing waters spelled deadly treachery for those foolish enough to enter them.

His eyes moved across the width of the Mississippi. Here and there, flotsam floated half-hidden by the water. Branches, trees, and even cargo crates bobbed in the current, thrust downriver like projectiles shot from firearms.

The gambler's reflections returned to the island and the cave. Did his three rafting companions still huddle there, waiting for the river to recede enough to once again begin their southward journey? He hoped the three had enough combined sense not to try their luck with the raft for at least another day or two. But with those three there was no way to tell.

A sad little smile touched his lips. What had been their reaction when they discovered him missing? It wouldn't take a genius to put one and one together and come up with the conclusion that he had discovered the skiff with its rather stiff occupant and somehow managed to fall into the river. From that point they would surely extrapolate that he had been swept away by the raging water and drowned.

The wrong conclusion, Chance admitted to himself, but nevertheless the one they would reach. And the same thing he would have concluded had he been in their position.

Wonder how they sent me off to my eternal reward? The gambler grinned. He was certain it hadn't been a solemn occasion of long faces, tears, and keening. More likely, they had caught a batch of catfish, fried them, and then while they stuffed their bellies with that sweet white meat, they had sat around the camp fire, lying about what a good man he been, each of them exaggerating his character to heroic proportions.

With an arched eyebrow and a nod, Chance recognized that just the opposite might have been true. The three might have decided to embellish on the roguish aspects of his life, creating the blackest scoundrel ever to walk this land. *A low-ranking duke shouldn't expect much better!*

A crash of brush from the river's edge drew the gambler from his morbid, mental wanderings. Below, he found the source of the noise—five logs, lashed together with rope, had crashed into a copse of poplar saplings that stood with their trunks half under the water. Better was the fact that the logs were snagged on the trees.

Chance knew it was just a matter of time before the current would wash the logs free. Pivoting, he ran back to the barn. In a feed room built at the front of the structure, he found what he wanted—a fifty-foot length of rope. Snatching it from the wooden peg it hung from, he sprinted back to the river.

Scrambling down the bank in a half slide, half walk, he carefully waded into the water. He moved one step at a time, making sure of his footing before each new step. He had spent one night in the floodwaters and had no desire to see if he could survive another.

The current washed around his upper thighs when he reached the poplars. He secured one end of the rope around three of the trunks before edging from the copse to the logs. He then looped and tied the other end of the rope about two of the logs. The fifty-foot length of the rope would ensure that the logs remained anchored to the bank in spite of the receding water. After giving both ends of the rope several tugs to make certain they would hold, he carefully picked his way back to the bank.

A wide grin rode on his face as he studied his unexpected prize. Like the raft he had ridden with his three companions, these logs had once been part of a larger logger's raft that had probably been torn away during the flood. More important, the five logs, if Sam Clemens hadn't been lying, could be sold. Which was exactly what the gambler intended to do with them tomorrow. Even if they brought only a dollar each in Ben Daniel, he would have the needed money for the telegram!

Chance whistled a few tortured strains of "Camptown Races" as he turned from the river and walked back to the barn. What had begun as a dreary evening had abruptly taken an upswing. It would take only two or three days for his attorney Philip Duwayne to wire him a few hundred dollars after he received the telegram. After that the gambler would purchase a new suit and book passage on the first riverboat heading southward.

Clothes? Chance glanced down at the trousers he wore. The wade in the river had left them spattered with mud and grime. A wave of guilt suffused the gambler. Leaving the Ragglin sisters with a load of dirty clothes wasn't the way to repay the kindness they had shown him.

After a trip to the clothesline to retrieve his own clothing and one to the well for a bucket of water, Chance reentered the barn. All he could find was a bar of amber saddle soap in the feed room, but soap was soap. He stripped away the dirty clothes he wore, and quickly bathed his own body. While he let the warm evening air dry his skin, he began to scrub the mud from the borrowed clothes.

With the task completed, he was dry enough to don his own pants for the trip across the farmyard to the clothesline where he hung the dripping shirt and pants. Back in the barn, he stretched out atop his pallet of straw and blankets and closed his eyes.

The rap of knuckles on wood came from the barn door. Then a feminine voice questioned, "Chance?"

"Caitlyn?" The gambler pushed to his elbows.

The door opened and Caitlyn entered, holding a chimneyed lamp above her head. The light from the burning wick bathed her in a soft yellow glow. The gambler arched an eyebrow; it took him several seconds before he realized that the young woman wore a white summer dress instead of the men's work clothes she had been in all day. The evening breeze carried the scent of soap and rose water as she stepped toward him.

"I heard you moving around out here," she said, "and wondered if you might like some company. Lizzy and Marybeth have already gone to bed, but I couldn't sleep."

Chance scooted to one side of the pallet and patted the other. Caitlyn took the offered seat without hesitation. "Pa used to like a cigar after dinner. I thought you might like the same."

The gambler accepted the cigar she held out and lit it with the lamp. He didn't even mind that it was a two-fer. After smoking Clemens's reclaimed cigars, it tasted like the finest of tobaccos.

While he smoked, they talked of their lives—Chance of the river and Caitlyn of the farm, her parents, and a young man named Tommy Bodine, who had left her with a promise to return from a war that cared little for a man's hastily made promises. It was when she spoke of her Uncle John and the tears misted her eyes as they had that morning that the gambler crushed what remained of the cigar under his boot and gently enclosed her in his arms.

Comfort was what he offered, so their kiss came as a surprise. Or perhaps he was lying to himself. Caitlyn hadn't bathed and donned a dress and sought him merely for conversation. Nor had he invited her to his bed to talk of the river and farming. Although neither had whispered of the needs of a man and woman, both had realized the reason for Caitlyn's visit.

When their lips parted, Chance's fingers found the buttons at the neck of her dress. A sharp, little gasp of anticipation escaped her lips as he worked the first from its eye, then easily slipped down the line that ran all the way to her waist.

His hands then parted the open dress. She wore nothing beneath except herself. She drew a long breath as his eyes caressed the uptilted forms of her delicate breasts. Small, like ripe, swollen apples, the two mounds of firm flesh thrust dark nipples toward the gambler. He bent and gently kissed the summery valley between those two peaks. Beneath the fragrances of soap and rose water was the warm aroma of woman.

Her hands moved to the back of his head, directing his lips to one of those tempting mounds. A shuddery gasp pushed from her throat as the tip of his tongue cajoled a nipple until it stood thick and aroused. Without further direction from the fingers that wove through the strands of his hair, he paid equal attention to the other nipple.

Eventually, she pulled his head from her breasts and once more covered his mouth with her lips. As their tongues sought and probed, their hands tugged and pulled at their clothing. A slight roll here, a lift of her legs, and her dress slid over her hips to be tossed carelessly aside. His trousers and boots presented a greater problem, but only for a few seconds while he stopped and yanked them off.

For a moment their eyes moved over each other's nakedness. Like her breasts, there was a delicate line to her body as though it were cast of fragile china. Her long, coltish legs seemed to stretch forever from the tips of her toes to a soft triangle of down between the union of her thighs.

The arms that reached up and pulled Chance back to the blankets were not those of a china doll. They were all woman and willing. While their mouths met again, their hands stroked, caressed, and explored. Another gasp pushed from her lips as her fingertips found him and traced over the full measure of his desire.

"It's been a long time since Tommy Bodine," she whispered as he came to her.

He needed no other words. In that simple sentence, she told him that although her body had known a man, she was not experienced in the ways of the flesh. He entered the moist haven of her body gently, tenderly. Then he remained motionless, allowing her time to accustom herself to him. When he moved, it was only when her pelvis began to undulate.

Slowly with a rocking rhythm, he reacquainted her with the pleasure of a man and woman. When her body at last released the passion that had been pent up within it ever since a young man had marched off to war, it was with cries of joy, and fingernails that bit deeply into his back.

Their second lovemaking was guided by far more fiery passion and brought his own equally fiery release. Their third ended with both of them wrapped in each other's arms and drifting into sleep.

ELEVEN

The soft, taunting insistence of Caitlyn's fingertips brought Chance from a restful sleep. His eyes blinked open to discover the young woman propped on an elbow gazing down at him. The smile on her face contained more than a friendly greeting.

He blinked again, surprised by the light in the barn. "Is it morning already?"

"We forgot to blow out the lamp," she said, leaning down to lightly kiss his lips. "But the roosters will be crowing in another hour. I have to get back into the house before then."

The gambler didn't question the reasons for her leaving; their names were Lizzy and Marybeth. An older sister had to set an example for her siblings. Being found in the hay with a man who was little more than a stranger wasn't the way to keep young sisters on the straight and narrow path.

"An hour, hmmmm?" Chance's left hand reached out to stroke up the silky texture of her thigh. His palm eased upward over the womanly flare of her hip and along her side until his fingers cupped beneath the firm upthrusted form of one of her breasts. His fingertips lightly kneaded the summery flesh while the pad of his thumb busied the nipple, bringing it to attention.

"At least an hour." Her lips brushed against his when she answered.

"Then we have more than enough time for this." He rolled her to her back in the straw and slid atop her when her thighs parted in invitation.

"I was hoping you would say that," she said as she reached down to guide him into the liquid warmth of her body.

There was no better way to start a day.

Chance followed Caitlyn from the barn. While she slipped back into the dark farmhouse, he drew a fresh bucket of water from the well and returned to the barn. After a quick bath to remove the sweat of their lovemaking from his body, he sat in the darkness, letting the air dry his skin. When the grays and purples of predawn glowed on the eastern horizon, he dressed and stretched atop his makeshift bed with his arms folded beneath his head.

The tantalizing aromas of baking biscuits, frying bacon, and brewing coffee wafted from the open rear door of the farmhouse, setting the gambler's stomach to rumbling for ten minutes before Marybeth knocked on the barn door and invited him to breakfast. Inside, the table was set for four. Lizzy was already at her place and Marybeth took hers as she waved Chance to the head of the table. Caitlyn, once more dressed in a man's work clothes, moved between stove and table with platters piled high with biscuits, bacon, and eggs.

Chance watched her, imagining, beneath those unflattering shirt and breeches, the woman who had so hungrily helped him greet the new day less than an hour ago. It wasn't a hard task. He wondered if either Lizzy or Marybeth noticed the rose blush on their sister's cheeks or the secretive little smile that uplifted the corners of her mouth. If they didn't, they were blind. Or was it just that he viewed the woman through new eyes?

"Will you be traveling farther downriver today, Chance?" Marybeth asked while she buttered a biscuit and spooned strawberry jam atop it.

The gambler nodded, washing down a mouthful of egg with a swig of black coffee. "At least to Ben Daniel."

From the corner of an eye he noticed Caitlyn's gaze dart to him. Her smile vanished in the batting of an eye.

"Last night I found five logs the flood washed onto the bank," he continued. "I thought that I would take them into town and sell them. They should bring enough for a telegram to New Orleans."

"Then you won't be leaving today?"

Caitlyn's voice held a touch too much eagerness. Both Lizzy and Marybeth glanced at their sister.

"Not until my attorney wires back some money," Chance replied.

"You're welcome to the use of our barn until then." This from Lizzy, who looked back at her older sister. "Isn't he, Caitlyn?"

"Chance is quite welcome to stay in the barn," she answered without glancing at the gambler. "I find it kind of a comfort having a man on the farm again."

The smile returned to the corners of her mouth, adding another level to her reply.

When her dark brown eyes did shift to Chance, she said, "I'll be going into Ben Daniel today myself. I have to trade the corn in the wagon at the general store."

"And?" Lizzy asked.

Caitlyn didn't answer, so Marybeth pressed: "Are you going to talk with Uncle John again?"

The oldest Ragglin sister pursed her lips and nodded. "Soon as I've dealt with the corn, I'll talk with him—not that I think it will do any good. Still, I'll talk with him."

Both the younger sisters fell silent, as did Chance. While he would have like to have helped the three women, he saw no way that he could. The fate of the farm rested with the sisters and their uncle.

"Chance," Caitlyn said, breaking the heavy silence, "you're welcome to ride back to the farm with me this afternoon."

He glanced up. "I appreciate that. Seven miles is a long way to walk if it isn't necessary."

"The wagon will be hitched at the general store," she said. "You can meet me there. Oh, Earlee Bodine owns the woodyard. He's the man you'll want to deal with over those logs. He drives a hard bargain, but he's a fair man."

Chance thanked her, silently wondering if Earlee was related to another Bodine named Tommy, who had foolishly left this beautiful, young woman to get himself killed in an equally foolish war.

Chance saw Caitlyn on her way to town before he borrowed an ax from the remaining sisters and walked to the riverbank. The floodwaters had rapidly receded during the night. The five logs, at the water's edge, strained at the end of their rope twenty-five feet from the poplar saplings that had snagged them last night.

The gambler said a silent thank-you for the rope's strength, then used the ax to hew through the trunk of one of the saplings. With the blade, he stripped away the branches and limbs. Grabbing the smaller end of the sapling, he braced the larger portion of the trunk against the ground and leaned heavily onto it. The sapling bowed a bit beneath his weight, but it didn't snap. Pleased with its strength, the gambler hefted it to a shoulder.

Unknotting the rope he had tied about the poplars last evening, he walked to the water's edge and pulled the raft to the shoreline. He tossed the rope atop the five logs, then leaped to the wood behind it.

The stripped sapling formed a perfect pole for the task at hand. Although the river's rage had diminished over the past days, a strong current remained that tried to suck him and the five logs out to the center of the Mississippi. Chance bent back and strained arms, using the makeshift pole to keep the logs close to the bank. Without a rudder on the small raft, he would have been completely at the mercy of the current should it ever have taken control.

An hour passed and then another before he sighted the village of Ben Daniel around a turn in the river. A large sign beyond a half-submerged, wooden pier that jutted out into the water read: BODINE'S WOODYARD FIREWOOD AND LUMBER FOR SALE AT REASONABLE PRICES.

Hoping Earlee Bodine was as reasonable about his purchasing price as he was about selling, Chance poled around the pier and worked the five logs toward the sign. Water had crept high into the riverfront yard and from all appearances had washed away at least 50 percent of Bodine's stock. A fact that could be twisted to work for both the buyer and the seller when it came down to the brass tacks of haggling.

Once past the pier, twenty strong strokes brought gambler and logs to the water's edge. Chance leaped to ground that was more mud than solid, and tied the raft to one of the poles that supported Bodine's sign. He found the owner of that sign inside a wooden shack at the front of the yard, sipping from a glass of buttermilk between bites of a sandwich constructed with a thick slab of ham slapped between two equally thick slices of bread.

"Name's Earlee Bodine." The man rose from his chair as the gambler entered the shack, wiped a hand on a thigh of his breeches, and held it out to the stranger. "How can I help you?"

"I was hoping that I might be able to help you," Chance said, deciding that a foot in the door was the best way to start negotiating the sale. "It appears you were hit pretty hard by the flood—"

"Damned near wiped me out and left me in the poorhouse," Bodine cut in before the gambler could finish. As though sensing a deal in the making, the man delivered his line with an appropriate long face and a weary shake of his head. "The river ain't hit me as bad since '60. I'll be hurtin' for six months to a year—if I don't fold and go under first."

"As long as a man's got a good supply of wood, he can survive on the Mississippi," Chance answered to counter Bodine's defense. "And what I have are five prime quality logs suited for board or firebox."

Bodine scratched at his chin, cast another downtrodden look at the gambler, then nodded. "Let's take a gander at your merchandise."

The woodyard owner arched a questioning eyebrow

when he saw the five logs. "You ain't got the looks of a logger about you, friend. Yet, it's plain to see them logs are part of a logger's raft."

"You've a good eye, Mr. Bodine," Chance answered, making no attempt to lie. "I found them washed ashore upriver. Since they don't have anyone's name on them, I thought that I might as well claim them."

Bodine nodded and scratched his chin again. "Give you four bits a piece for 'em."

Thus it began in earnest. Chance countered with five dollars a log. Bodine upped the offer to seventy-five cents, once more emphasizing that the flood had all but wiped his yard from the face of the earth. The gambler replied that he recognized the situation, but without wood the yard might as well have been wiped from the face of the earth, and lowered his selling price by a quarter. For an hour the two alternated in raising and lowering their respective offers until a price of two dollars a log was struck and sealed with a handshake. Two dollars was less than Chance expected, but more than enough for the telegram, so he was satisfied. Two dollars was more than Bodine had expected to pay, but less than the logs' value, so a smile hung at the corners of his mouth.

Back in the shack Chance slipped ten silver dollars in his coat pocket and asked directions to the telegraph office. Bodine stood in the doorway and pointed to a small, white-washed building a quarter of a mile from his yard. "Willy Joe ought to be back from lunch by now."

Thanking the man, the gambler picked his way down a muddy street to the building. He opened a door beneath a shingle sign that proclaimed this to be the Telegraph Office. Willy Joe was a rail-thin man who leaned back in a chair and stared out a window that opened on Ben Daniel's main street. Chance saw only one wagon rolling down the muddy avenue and could only wonder what held the man's attention so.

Working a wad of chewing tobacco that made his left cheek appear as though it concealed a baseball, the telegra-

pher eventually turned from window to gambler. He spat a
dark stream of juice into a tin can on the floor beside the
chair before he asked, "How can I help you?"

Since the man was sitting in a telegraph office and was
supposedly a telegrapher, there weren't too many ways he
could "help" a stranger. For a moment Chance considered
telling him that he was here to purchase a team of horses,
but let it slide; the answer would be lost on Willy Joe.

"Telegram to New Orleans," the gambler said.

Willy Joe handed him a pad of paper and a pencil. "Just
write down what you want sent. You might keep it short
since I have to charge by the word."

The telegrapher emphasized his last comment by giving
Chance the once-over as though the gambler's clothes indicated an inability to pay.

Chance took pad and pencil and wrote, "Broke and
stranded in Ben Daniel, Arkansas. Send $500—Chance."
He then wrote the address of his attorney Philip Duwayne
at the top of the paper before handing it back to Willy Joe.

The telegrapher scanned the message, pursed his lips,
and said, "That'll be three dollars and fifty cents."

"Three fifty!" Chance stared at the man. "Upriver in
Kentucky the same message cost only three dollars!"

"That was Kentucky and this is Arkansas" was the only
explanation Willy Joe offered. "Three dollars and fifty
cents."

Mumbling a curse beneath his breath the gambler dug in
his coat pocket and extracted four of the silver dollars Earlee Bodine had paid him and dropped them onto Willy
Joe's extended palm.

After returning Chance's fifty cents change, the telegrapher sat down at his key and quickly fired off the message
in a series of electronic dots and dashes. Thirty seconds
after his finger left the key, a burst of clatter came from the
telegraph. Willy Joe looked up at Chance and grinned.
"Little Rock received your wire. Lucky you brought it in
when you did. They'll relay it down to Baton Rouge and
then to New Orleans by this evening. If your friend is

quick to answer, you should have this draft in two or three days. It takes a bit more time to clear money along the way."

After nearly two weeks on the river floating on a raft, two or three days didn't seem too bad, especially now that Chance had money in his pockets. Thanking the telegrapher, he turned and opened the door.

"Where should I send the answer when it comes?" Willy Joe called after him.

Chance considered giving the Ragglin farm as his address, then realized that after the auction tomorrow there would be no Ragglin farm. "I'll check with you every afternoon."

Willy Joe nodded his acceptance as Chance once more turned and left. Outside, the gambler stared down Ben Daniel's main street. Two signs caught his eye. One marked the general store, where Caitlyn's wagon and mules were hitched to the rail that ran before the store. The second was to a saloon about four doors down from the general store.

Chance's immediate reaction was to head straight for the saloon and see if he could find a friendly poker game and swell the six-fifty in his pocket back to the original ten. He took ten steps toward the saloon, before changing his mind. He had promised Caitlyn that he would meet her at the general store. After the rendezvous, he would move on to the gaming tables and try his luck.

The general store was empty, except for a clerk who placed bottles of "Dr. Sarrantonio's Liniment and Purgative" atop a case of shelves behind the store's counter.

"Caitlyn Ragglin was in here about a half hour back," the clerk answered the gambler's inquiry. "Your name don't happen to be Chance Sharpe does it?"

Chance nodded.

"Then she left a message for you," the man continued. "She said to say that she was going to meet with her Uncle John, and if you wanted a ride back to the farm, you was to wait out by the wagon 'til she got back."

The gambler thanked the clerk and left a message that Caitlyn could find him in the saloon when she returned. Chance then walked down the street and pushed through the batwing doors at the saloon's entrance. The establishment's only patrons, including a bartender with a white apron around his waist, sat at a table near the saloon's door. All five were engrossed in the cards they held in their hands.

Chance's gaze went to the pot at the center of the table. Pennies and nickels were the only coins that could be seen. He didn't mind; a man with only six dollars and fifty cents in his pocket didn't complain about low stakes.

"Gentlemen," he began as the five finished their hand, "I was wondering if you'd mind a stranger sitting in on this game?"

The clock on the wall read four-thirty in the afternoon, when Chance raked a fifty-cent pot from the center of the table. Two of the players pushed away from the game, announcing it was drawing near to suppertime, and they should be moseying home. The bartender also abandoned his chair, saying he had to prepare for the evening's patrons.

With only three players left, poker was out of the question, so Chance suggested a few hands of blackjack. The two men still at the table shook their heads, preferring to sip at flat beers rather than change games.

The gambler lifted his piles of pennies and nickels from the table and traded them in for six silver dollars at the bar. With the remaining five nickels, he bought a shot of bourbon—at least that's what the bottle read. It seared his throat like two-day-old moonshine with a touch of boot polish added to give it color.

He didn't complain. In four hours he had increased his bank roll to twelve dollars—almost double the amount in his pocket when he walked into the saloon. And more than enough to sustain him until Philip Duwayne wired the five hundred he had requested in the telegram.

Waving away the bartender when he approached with an open bottle to refill the gambler's empty glass, Chance walked back outside and returned to the general store where Caitlyn's wagon still waited.

"She ain't been in here since you first came lookin' for her," the clerk informed him. "But 'bout an hour ago or so, I saw her and a man cross the street to Clare Waylon's cafe. Haven't seen either of them come out."

Chance nodded his head in thanks, and looked up and down the street. The cafe was across the street, two doors down. It was as good a place as any to meet Caitlyn. He might even convince her to allow him to treat her to dinner.

His hand closed around the cafe's doorknob, and he froze. Through the cafe's window he saw Caitlyn seated at a table with a man. But that man wasn't her Uncle John. It was Brad Calloway!

Chance forced his fingers to release the doorknob. He stepped back, quelling his desire to burst into the cafe and confront Calloway. Something he would have done without hesitation had Caitlyn not been at that table.

Uncertain what was happening here, the gambler retreated across the street and waited beside the wagon. As soon as Caitlyn came out—Calloway was his!

TWELVE

Fifteen minutes passed with Chance waiting on the far side of the wagon, watching the cafe's windows out of the corners of his eyes. He tried to keep his back to the small restaurant as much as possible: if he recognized Calloway, he realized that the blond weasel might also recognize him. Until he was certain of what was going on here, he was quite happy with Calloway's being unaware of his presence in Ben Daniel.

Inside the cafe he saw Caitlyn and Calloway rise. However, only Caitlyn walked from the door. Her angry expression appeared to be carved in stone as she crossed the street in determined strides, giving no heed to the mud she splattered onto her pants.

"Come on, let's get out of here." She tilted her head to the gambler when she noticed him by the wagon.

Before she could climb to the driver's board, Chance grabbed her arm and spun her about to face him. Her eyes narrowed to slits that barely contained the flames of rage burning in their depths. "What do you think you're doing?"

"That man in the cafe"—Chance jerked his head toward the restaurant "—who was he?"

"Who do you think he was?" Caitlyn stared at him in disbelief. "That was my Uncle John. Now get your hands off me and get into the wagon, if you're going back to the farm for the night."

"That man's name isn't Uncle John." The gambler's hand remained clamped firmly around her arm. He still didn't know exactly what was happening here, but he could guess. "That's Brad Calloway sitting in there."

"Who?" Confusion washed over Caitlyn's face. "What are you talking about?"

"Brad Calloway—the bastard that threw me over the side of the *Gulf Runner*." Chance tried to remember the abbreviated version of his "great adventure" that he had told her and couldn't recall what facts he had omitted. That was the problem with lying, or half lying—it was damned hard to keep a story straight.

Caitlyn blinked, stared at the gambler, looked at the cafe, then stared at Chance again. When she spoke, her words came from her lips with uncertain hesitancy. "You mean that man isn't my Uncle John Seese?"

John Seese! The image of a corpse lying in the bottom of a skiff thrust itself into the gambler's mind. He mentally rolled the dead man to his back and stared at the dark bullet hole in the center of his forehead. Chance once more slipped a wallet from the corpse's coat and read the name on the soggy letters tucked away there—John Seese of New York City. The ugly pieces began to tumble into their places.

"Chance, what are you talking about? I tell you that the man sitting in there is my uncle," Caitlyn persisted.

"I haven't time to explain now. But that isn't John Seese. You'll have to trust me for now." The gambler lifted her to the driver's board. "I want you to drive the team to the edge of town and wait for me. One way or the other, I'll be along within the hour."

He unhitched the mules as she lifted the reins. She started to question him again, but he shook his head and popped one of the animals on its rump with the flat of his hand. Mules, wagon, and driver moved down Ben Daniel's muddy main street.

Chance turned to the cafe. He wasn't certain exactly what had happened, but he could put two and two together and come up with an ugly picture. John Seese hadn't put a bullet through his own skull, but the gambler could damned well guess who had placed a gun to his head.

He had crossed half the street when he halted. Four burly men walked from a narrow alley beside the cafe and moved through the restaurant's door. Inside, Calloway stood to greet them. The five laughed in obvious delight.

The gambler stepped to the side to avoid notice. The men weren't the four apes Calloway had with him aboard the *Gulf Runner*—the blond weasel had permanently disposed of that foursome—but these four could have been brothers of the original team of trained gorillas. The difference was that these four carried pistols tucked beneath their belts rather than lengths of lead pipe.

Chance moved farther to the side to make certain none of the men saw him. He had no idea who the four were, but it was more than apparent that they were friends of the blond weasel, who waved them to a table and sat down with them. Perhaps they were the very friends whose money Calloway had lost to the gambler aboard the *Gulf Runner*. Chance could only guess at their identity.

The one thing that he *was* certain of was that he would have to postpone facing Calloway. Five-to-one odds weren't bad in a horse race, but in a fight, they could be deadly, especially when the five were all packing pistols and the one was armed only with his fists.

Withdrawing, Chance crossed the street, then moved toward the edge of town where Caitlyn waited.

As the wagon rolled toward the Ragglin farm, Chance began at the beginning with Calloway and his four goons coldcocking Clemens and him and tossing them over the railing of the *Gulf Runner*. This time he left no detail unsaid, especially of his witnessing Calloway murder a man aboard the crippled riverboat and of his discovering the body in the skiff.

"The man in that skiff was middle aged," Chance said. "Calloway can't be more than thirty."

Caitlyn nibbled at her lower lip and nodded. "I was bothered by Uncle John's age at first, but he was only Pa's half brother, and he *did* have all the letters and papers."

"And you had never seen him before," Chance concluded for her. "You aren't to blame, Caitlyn. This man makes ruthlessness a profession."

"And you think he killed my Uncle John?" she asked.

"That's the way it adds up to me," Chance replied. "I'm just grabbing at thin air on some of this, but I'd say John Seese was a passenger aboard the *Gulf Runner*. He and Calloway met each other and started talking, maybe over a drink or two in the main cabin. A man on a long journey will tell a total stranger things about himself that he would never consider mentioning under normal circumstances. It's lonesome and boring aboard a paddlewheeler most of the time. People try to make friends to help pass the time."

"And Uncle John told this Brad Calloway why he was traveling to Arkansas?" Caitlyn asked.

Chance nodded. "Calloway saw a way to pull a scam and walk away with your inheritance, plus the money he would get for the farm when it sold. The night Calloway and his four apes scuttled the *Gulf Runner* was probably when John Seese was killed. The confusion of a boat going down would cover a single gunshot easy enough."

"But why would Calloway leave my uncle's wallet on his body?" Caitlyn turned to the gambler and frowned. "Especially when there were letters in it that could identify him?"

"As well as fifty dollars." Chance shook his head. "That's what's got me puzzled. My guess is Calloway didn't mean to leave the wallet on him. I suspect that he killed John Seese and dumped his body into a skiff to get it out of the way, planning to search it later. The papers and letters he has with him now came out of Seese's stateroom. Before Calloway could get back to the body, the *Gulf Runner* broke up and the skiff slipped away."

Chance paused and mentally ran over everything he had pieced together. There were holes here and there, but he was willing to wager the scenario was 90 percent accurate. "What I don't understand is where the four men I saw with Calloway came from."

"They were with him when he arrived in Ben Daniel," Caitlyn answered. "I asked him about them, and he said he had hired them to protect the money we would be taking north with us."

A dry chuckle pushed past the gambler's lips and he shook his head again. "Apparently Calloway hasn't done much business with banks in his life. A banker would simply transfer funds from the bank here in Ben Daniel to his own bank in New York. Calloway's sloppy, and that's to our advantage. If we're going to stop him, we have to arrange it so he trips himself."

"Trips himself?" Caitlyn's brow furrowed. "Chance, what are you talking about?" She pulled back on the reins, halting the team of mules. "You've told me enough. We're going back into town and tell all this to the sheriff. He'll do the stopping."

Chance reached out and took Caitlyn's hand, squeezing it. "It's not that simple. We've no proof to support anything that I've told you. Without your uncle's body, as far as the law is concerned Brad Calloway is John M. Seese."

"But everything that happened to you and everything you saw will be enough to convince the sheriff," she protested.

"It'll come down to his word against mine, Caitlyn. Take a good look at me, and then tell me who you'd believe if you were in the sheriff's place."

Her dark eyes moved over the gambler. Her expression said everything. Chance's tattered suit bespoke of a worthless drifter willing to fabricate an outlandish story in the hope of making off with a portion of the Ragglin sisters' inheritance.

Caitlyn lifted the reins and clucked the mules forward, moving toward the farm.

A note on the kitchen table from Lizzy explained that she and Marybeth had retired for the night, leaving supper out for Caitlyn and Chance, should he return to the farm.

Caitlyn removed the old newspapers covering the bowls

and plates, neatly folded them, and placed them atop a counter. Biscuits, mashed potatoes, fried chicken, and still warm cream gravy was the evening's fare. They ate in silence. Chance supposed her mind wandered the same path as his—Brad Calloway and how to stop him before the farm was auctioned tomorrow. He also assumed that she had reached the same conclusion he did—there was no way.

As Chance finished the last piece of chicken on his plate, Caitlyn rose and left the kitchen to return with blankets and a pillow. The gambler didn't ask what they were for. He took them from her arms, lightly kissed her lips, and walked out to the barn.

After drawing a bucket of water from the well and bathing, he spread the blankets on his straw bed and stretched atop them. Sleep refused to come. Although he admitted he was unable to stop Calloway, there had to be some way to tangle the blond weasel in his own mistakes.

Wishing he had another of Caitlyn's father's cigars to help him think, he folded his arms beneath his head and stared into the barn's darkness above him. If they had a few more days, the situation might be different. Once the money arrived from Philip in New Orleans, he'd have a new suit of clothes and cash in his pocket. No longer would he be a penniless drifter.

He realized that a lawman wouldn't be inclined to believe his story any more then than now, but at least he was certain he could get the sheriff to check it out—a man who could wire New Orleans for five hundred dollars and receive it usually was listened to.

It would take time, but even without John Seese's body, there were ways to prove his story. Booking agents kept records of passengers that would place him aboard the *Gulf Runner* along with Seese and Calloway. And there must have been survivors when the riverboat went down. Any of those men who had played poker with Calloway could identify him.

As well as some of the boat's officers and crew, Chance

thought, realizing stewards were quick to learn passengers and their names: it meant bigger tips.

The gambler shook his head. He was wasting time considering something that would never be. His money from New Orleans wouldn't arrive in Ben Daniel for two or three more days. By then Calloway would be long gone, his pockets stuffed with every penny the Ragglin sisters had.

What he needed was something that he could use against Calloway tomorrow before the farm went up for auction. But what?

That question repeated itself in his mind, when he heard the creak of an opening door. The yellow light of lamp preceded Caitlyn into the barn. She walked to the stall and sat beside him on the blankets.

"You can't get him off your mind either, can you?" she asked.

"He's all I've been thinking about," the gambler admitted.

"There's no way we can stop him, is there?"

"I haven't given up hope." Chance sat up. He took the lamp from her hand and placed it on the stall's floor. He then wrapped her in his arms and held her tightly. She shuddered against his chest, tears of frustration rolling down her cheeks. He pulled her closer to him.

"If only Pa had left some money buried in a tin can," she said as the tears subsided. "I'd give it to you, and let you bid on the farm tomorrow. Calloway would get away with the money, but at least we'd still have the land. That's what matters: with the farm, Marybeth, Lizzy, and I can still make a life for ourselves."

Her words set something wiggling at the back of the gambler's mind. That elusive something refused to be pinned down and defined. Try as he did, he couldn't bring it into focus.

Caitlyn didn't help any when her face lifted, and she kissed his lips. "Chance," she whispered when they parted, "I need you tonight. I need to be held and loved."

He didn't question her reasons, but cupped her face in his palms and kissed her. Together their hands freed the buttons and hooks of their clothing until they lay side by side on the blankets, warm flesh pressed to warm flesh.

As gentle as he had been the night before, he doubled that care tonight. His hands stroked over the silken texture of her body, smoothing away the trembles of fear and doubt. When his lips and tongue left her mouth, it was to tenderly kiss down the arch of her neck and taunt over her bare shoulders.

Slowly, leaving no inch of her body untouched by his brushing lips and flicking tongue, he followed a meandering route that eventually led to the crests of her upthrust breasts. There he paused to reintroduce himself to the plump buds of flesh perched atop those creamy mounds. When both dark cherries stood stiffly erect, his mouth slid to the warm valley separating the twin knolls.

He kissed downward over her fluttering stomach, past the sensual well of her navel. A moan of uninhibited desire writhed from her lips as she parted her thighs to admit him to his final destination.

Teasing fingertips and laving tongue were all he needed to unleash cries of ecstasy. While her body quaked and trembled from released desire, he slid atop her, their bodies joining as one. Her legs lifted, heels locking behind his calves, as they gently rocked together in a rhythm as old as the first man and woman.

When her cries of passion rose again, they were chorused by his own moans of fiery release. Then they lay there, neither wishing to break the union they had achieved, until the last quiver of passion passed. Rolling from her, he held her close, listening to the rhythm of breathing gentle into the softness of sleep.

An hour after Caitlyn drifted off, Chance eased his arm from beneath her head and slipped from her side. Again wishing for a cigar to help focus his thoughts, he stepped outside.

The moon rode high in the sky, testifying to the early hour of the night. Calloway and his four goons were probably in the Ben Daniel's saloon lifting mugs of beer and congratulating themselves on the money that would be theirs tomorrow.

Money to buy the farm: Caitlyn's earlier suggestion pushed to the forefront of the gambler's thoughts. If he had the money, he would use it to buy the farm for the sisters. He had loaned money on shakier business deals than this land in the past. With Caitlyn's dedication to the farm, he was certain the loan would prove a good one.

The snag to those thoughts was that the only person in town with money enough to cover the farm was Brad Calloway. Chance drew a heavy breath. *My money, dammit!*

He straightened; a smile played at the corners of his mouth. That elusive thought wiggled free and emerged from the back of his mind. His smile transformed into a grin. There were a lot of "ifs" to the scheme that began to solidify in his mind. But "ifs" were better than sitting on his backside and letting Calloway get away with his scam.

Inside the feed room, he found a pair of mane shears hung on the wall. Taking the shears, he crept into the farmhouse and picked up the newspaper Caitlyn had neatly folded and set aside before their dinner. The shears made short work of the paper. He stuffed the results in a pocket and returned to the barn. There he took a bridle from the feed room and placed it on one of the mules. He didn't bother with a saddle. Swinging to the animal's bare back, he rode into the night for Ben Daniel.

THIRTEEN

Chance tugged back on the reins. The strong-willed mule's neck bowed and its head swung side to side, fighting the bit. Twenty feet beyond the point the gambler had begun the process of halting the stubborn animal, it came to a begrudging standstill, then snorted its displeasure with the man astride its back.

While keeping a tight rein on the mule, Chance peered down Ben Daniel's main street—main relegated to the north—south running avenue because of two semiformed streets that stood to the west. A sprinkling of yellow-glowing light came from windows scattered over the Arkansas community. For the most part, these came from homes.

Only three lights burned along the main street. The first hung above the opened doors to a livery stable. The second barely lit the front window of the general store. So soft was this glow that the gambler discounted it to the owner working late over his books rather than being open. The brightest glare came from the center of the street—the saloon.

As good a place as any to begin, Chance decided, tapping the mule's side with his heels.

The animal remained motionless, except for a twitch of its long ears.

The gambler's heels rose and fell a second time with decided determination. The reply was another snort from his mount. A third, well-placed kick to the flanks brought the mule to life: it clomped forward at a leisurely pace more suited to pulling a plow than carrying a rider. But it did move, and for the moment that was enough.

In spite of the seven-mile ride into town, Chance's plan of action was no more solidified in his mind than it had been when he had left the Ragglin farm. Before he could employ the newspaper stuffed in his pocket, he had to locate Brad Calloway. And that might prove a problem, since all he knew of the man's whereabouts was that Caitlyn had once mentioned that her Uncle John had refused to stay at the farm upon his arrival in Ben Daniel, preferring a boardinghouse.

Surely there can't be more than one boardinghouse in this town, the gambler thought as the mule plodded down the street toward the saloon's lights. If Calloway wasn't inside, then all he had to do was inquire from one of the patrons about getting a room for the night. Should there prove to be more than one boardinghouse in Ben Daniel, then he would have to play the next step in his scheme by ear.

Using his full weight against the reins, the gambler managed to bring the mule to a halt before a hitching rail outside a barbershop to the left of the saloon. The individual hitching posts with their wrought-iron rings that lined the front of the saloon were occupied by saddled horses. The din of barroom conversation, an occasional boisterous laugh, and the clink of glasses came from within.

Chance frowned as he slid from the back of the mule and tied one of the reins around the rail. He had to mentally back-count the days before he understood the reason for so many patrons making use of the saloon's pleasures this night. It was Friday, and the still-high moon said that the night was young.

The gambler also understood why Calloway had set the farm's auction for the next day. A Saturday would ensure that farmers from throughout the area would be in town— all interested in acquiring additional acreage, if the price was right.

Pushing through the batwings, Chance walked straight to the bar, found an empty spot, and ordered a nickel beer. The brew was as hot as the summer night, but he offered no complaints. Slowly sipping from the mug gave him the opportunity to scan the saloon's patrons in the mirror that hung behind the bar.

His pulse doubled its tempo on his second pass over the men crowded into the saloon. Brad Calloway sat at a poker game with six other players on the far side of the room. The gambler's eyes narrowed when he noticed the small tower of greenbacks on the table in front of the man. *My money!*

Calloway located, Chance once more perused the patrons' faces in the mirror. He found the latest recruits to Calloway's gorilla-brigade strategically stationed around the room, as though purposely placed there in case of trouble.

The gambler couldn't imagine any man in the room causing trouble; most were dressed as farmers. And the last thing he wanted this night was trouble. His goal was money!

"Friend"—a man in a ragged straw hat to the gambler's right nudged his arm—"you ain't happened to have a spare chaw on ya, do ya?"

Chance glanced at the man, uncertain he had caught his words.

"I'm plumb out and sure could make use of a good chaw right now," the man went on.

When the gambler shook his head, the man pushed back his straw hat, scratched at his forehead, shrugged, and turned to the man on his other side. "Friend, I don't reckon you happened to have a spare chaw on ya, do ya? I could do with a good chaw long about now."

When the second man also shook his head, straw-hat's gaze wandered up and down the bar as though searching for a likely prospect to tap for a chew of tobacco. Before he sighted a pigeon, a third man approached from the back, slapped him on the shoulder, and asked, "Jim Bob, you ain't happened to have a spare chaw on ya, do ya?"

Chance gave his head a shake and turned away from what was obviously some unrecorded Arkansas tobacco ritual, and found Calloway's reflection in the mirror again, while watching the four goons out of the corners of his eyes.

A second table of card players sat on the opposite side of the room. While the first table tossed greenbacks into the pot, the second bet with pennies, nickels, and dimes. The gambler smiled, noticing an empty chair at that second table. If he was going to spend the evening keeping tabs on Calloway, he might as well make use of the twelve silver dollars in his pocket. With half a mug of beer in hand, he walked from the bar to the table.

Four kings brought Chance a pot totaling six bits and increased his original twelve dollars to fourteen twenty-five. It wasn't much of a profit to show for three hours at the table, but then pennies, nickels, and dimes weren't what he was after tonight.

What he was after, Calloway stuffed into a wallet as he bid the players at his table a good-night, and began to weave his way to the saloon's exit. From the corners of the room, four apes in human disguise trudged after him.

The five men had reached the door by the time Chance excused himself and raked his winnings from the table. Trying to ignore the race of his pulse, the gambler moved to the batwings and stepped outside. While he mounted the mule, he watched the five walk toward the livery stable. Tugging the animal's head around, Chance applied heels to flanks. The mule moved forward, following the five men at the safe distance of a block.

Outside the livery stable, they stopped. Chance resisted the urge to pull up his mount and wait to see what they did next. Instead he plodded down the street, catching the men's glances as he passed, head tucked low to his chest to keep his face in the shadows.

"See you in the morning," he heard Calloway say. "Make certain the horses are saddled and waiting as soon as . . ."

The blond weasel's voice trailed off as the gambler rode

past, turning the mule into an alley a block from the stable. Chance rode to the opposite end of the alley and stopped.

No homes stood on Ben Daniel's main street. If Calloway intended to spend this night in a boardinghouse, he had to walk to the next street.

Three minutes later Calloway emerged from behind the stable. He turned left, away from the mule and its rider. Half a block away, he walked into a two-story house.

Chance caught his breath. Not once as he had gone over the plan in his mind had he considered entering a room on a second floor. His eyes scanned the area around the house. There were no trees . . .

The gambler released his breath in a gust of relief. The glow of a lamp lit a window in the lower floor near the back of the house. He smiled. He now knew the location of Calloway's bedroom: all he had to do was wait.

The moon's movement through the heavens told the gambler that two hours had passed. Chance slid from the mule's back and tied a rein around a drainpipe that ran down the building beside him. For half the time he had waited, he had considered simply riding up to the house and hitching the mule outside. He had discarded the idea. A man on foot made little noise and was less likely to draw the attention of any of Ben Daniel's residents who suffered from insomnia tonight.

In spite of the fact that he walked from the alley as though he belonged on the street at this late hour, he felt like a thief in the night as he approached the two-story boardinghouse. Telling himself that he was merely going to reclaim money that was rightfully his didn't help.

If he were caught in the act, the authorities in this town were highly unlikely to view his act as anything other than burglary. *Which means,* he thought as he stopped outside the house, *you don't let yourself get caught.*

After a hasty check in all directions to make certain he went unseen, he slipped to the house's side and edged toward the window that had lit up when Calloway had entered. A smile uplifted the corners of his mouth when he reached his destination. The window was raised high to admit what little breeze stirred the warm summer night. Inside came the sound of snoring.

Giving his surroundings one last glance to check for eyes that might be following him, he carefully eased through the window. Inside, he stepped into a shadow and waited for his eyes to grow accustomed to the house's darkness, as well as giving his heart time to slow its runaway pounding.

Moonlight bathed Calloway's face as the man continued to snore, undisturbed by the intruder who had slipped into his bedroom. Chance considered the myriad of ways his fists could rearrange the man's features before he was fully awake, then set aside thoughts of revenge. He was here for the money and the money only. Calloway would have to wait until another day.

The man's clothing was draped over a chair five feet to the gambler's right. Taking one step at a time, Chance crossed to the chair. The wallet wasn't in the coat where he had seen Calloway stuff it before leaving the saloon. Nor was it in his trousers.

Where? Chance's gaze moved over the bedroom. Except for the chair and a small, drawerless table, the room was bare of furniture. There wasn't even a closet or standing butler in which to hang clothes.

Which means he has it in the bed with him.

Silently mouthing a curse that pertained to Calloway's parental relationship to a female mongrel, Chance turned and stared at the sleeping man. Unless he wore a money belt, the gambler gave himself odds that the wallet lay beneath the pillow, securely nestled under Calloway's head.

Or maybe not that securely. The gambler moved beside the bed. With his right hand, he reached out and slowly slid his hand beneath the pillow. Three inches in, he touched leather. Equal caution guided his movements as he gradually pulled the wallet from its hiding place.

With the moonlight that filtered through the open win-

dow bathing the wallet, he opened it and quickly extracted
the bills within. From his coat pocket, he pulled the pieces
of newspaper he had cut in the Ragglin kitchen. Sandwich-
ing the newspaper between two fifty-dollar bills, he substi-
tuted a worthless wad of paper for the bankroll he had
taken.

Just as he started to slide the wallet back under the pillow, Calloway flopped to his side and grunted. The man's
lips smacked wetly several times before he resumed his
snoring.

The gambler softly released an overly-held breath and
gently eased the wallet into its hiding place. Patting the
money in his coat, Chance exited the bedroom via the window. Two minutes later he was once again astride the
mule's bare back, riding for a farm he hoped to save.

Leaving the mule tied outside, Chance slipped into the
barn. Her sleep undisturbed by either his departure or arrival, Caitlyn lay stretched atop the blankets, her body de-
liciously naked. The gambler moved beside her, knelt, and
lightly kissed her left ear.

"Mmmm." She shifted a bit, her left hand giving a half-
hearted bat at the ear as though to brush away a fly.

When he kissed her a second time, his tongue gently
flicked at her earlobe.

She stirred again, her eyes opening to sleepy slits as she
rolled to the gambler and snuggled against him. "Huh?"
Her eyes widened in question. She peered up at his face,
doubt wrinkling her brow. "You're dressed? Where are you
going?"

"Been," he corrected and planted a long, smacking kiss
on her lips.

"Been?" Puzzlement still clouded her features when
they parted. "What do you mean?"

"While you've been lying here sawing logs, I took a
little ride into town." He grinned down at her.

"Ladies don't snore," she said with a pout.

Ladies also don't sneak into the barn for a roll in the

hay, he thought, but said, "However, a certain man imper-
sonating John M. Seese does. Quite loudly actually. Didn't
even notice when I slipped his wallet out from under his
pillow."

"Chance, you didn't!" Caitlyn's confusion deepened for
an instant, then was replaced by a broad grin as it dawned
on her what he was talking about. "You did, didn't you?
You did it!"

The gambler pulled the wad of bills from his pocket and
waved them under her nose. "In through his bedroom window, then out again. Only, I was carrying this when I left."

"Let me see!" Her voice held a childlike quality as he
handed her the bankroll. "I don't believe this. I don't believe it!"

Her tone was more credulous when she finished counting the bills. "Twenty-one hundred dollars!"

"About two hundred short of what Calloway took off of
me that night on the *Gulf Runner,*" he said. "But it should
be enough to make certain you don't lose this farm tomorrow."

"You mean you intend to give this to me?"

"Lend it." He shook his head. "I'll collect the interest
from Calloway in my own way, before I let the law take the
rest out of his hide."

"Chance"—her head moved from side to side in disbelief—"I don't know how my sisters and I will ever be able
to thank you."

The gambler tossed away his coat and began unbutton-
ing his shirt. "I don't know about Marybeth and Lizzy, but
I have an idea in mind for you."

Her eyes burned with an inner fire as she watched him
skin away his pants and come to her.

FOURTEEN

An hour before first light Chance and Caitlyn awoke. While the young woman slipped into the farmhouse to continue the chaste charade for her younger sisters, Chance used the time to bathe in another bucket of water drawn from the well. He dressed and waited to be summoned to breakfast with the three sisters.

The morning meal felt more like a funeral than the beginning of a new summer's day. Neither Lizzy nor Marybeth spoke while they set the table and settled into their places. Their long faces and distant expressions said they carried the full weight of the morning on their shoulders. Today they would lose their father's land, and no miracle to change the inevitable was in sight.

Actually, the miracle they yearned for sat within the slightly bulging pocket of the gambler's coat pocket. However, neither Caitlyn nor Chance mentioned the money. The decision to keep the secret cache from the two younger sisters had been Caitlyn's—one with which the gambler agreed. To reveal Chance's scheme to save the farm presented too many possibilities for slipups. Should either of the younger women greet their "Uncle John" with a smile today, or even a tone of voice that was too light, Calloway might grow suspicious.

And weasels alerted to danger are capable of anything, Chance thought, remembering how Calloway had dealt with his five companions aboard the *Gulf Runner*. He didn't doubt the man would employ these methods to extricate himself from a tight situation here, if he felt a trap closing in on him.

"I'm not up to fixing much of a breakfast this morning." Caitlyn slid a platter of biscuits onto the table beside butter and honey that already sat there. "Coffee and biscuits is it. If you want more, you'll have to cook it yourself."

Lizzy and Marybeth nodded in acceptance without glancing at their older sister as she filled four cups with coffee. Chance silently congratulated Caitlyn for playing her role so well, but his stomach rumbled in protest. For him it had been a very busy night both in Ben Daniel and in the barn. The gambler felt like he could devour a side of beef and about three dozen eggs, as well as every biscuit on the platter.

He kept his gnawing hunger to himself. Imitating the sisters' woeful silence, he ate half a dozen biscuits dripping with butter and honey, and washed them down with three cups of black coffee. It was enough to quiet his stomach, but left him feeling as though he had only nibbled at a tray of appetizers and still waited for the main course to be served.

"Lizzy, Marybeth," Caitlyn said as her sisters finished their single biscuits, "I know it will be hard, but I want us to look our best today. There'll be folks here from all over the county—people we've known all our lives. I don't want them to see us crying and bellowing. We'll do Ma and Pa proud by standing straight and tall."

The two sisters didn't answer, only nodded.

"Now go on upstairs and get rid of those work clothes and put on your Sunday finest," Caitlyn ordered. "I'll be along shortly."

Lizzy and Marybeth pushed from the kitchen table and left the room without question. Caitlyn turned to Chance and shook her head. She whispered, "It breaks my heart to see them like that—not knowing what we know."

"It's the only way." The gambler reached across the table and squeezed her hand. "Once the auction is over, they'll understand."

She drew a breath and nodded. "I know, but it's hard not to bust out and tell them about the money." Her hand returned the gambler's squeeze. "I know what we're supposed to do, but what about you? Is there anything I can do to help you?"

"I could use your father's razor and shaving mug." Chance ran a hand over his cheeks. "I'd also like to borrow some of your father's clothes again."

Caitlyn arched an eyebrow in question.

Chance shrugged. "I doubt that Calloway will be able to recognize me in these." He glanced down at his fraying suit. "But if I appear to be just another farmer interested in land, it will be safer."

The young woman tilted her head in acceptance. "Wait here, and I'll get you what you need."

While Caitlyn left to retrieve the required items, Chance buttered the remaining six biscuits on the platter, spread them with honey, and then neatly bundled them in a napkin, which he stuffed in a coat pocket. The auction was scheduled for straight-up noon: the cold biscuits would be the only lunch he got today.

There were three things that he had learned while in the army—a man had to eat, sleep, and relieve himself whenever the opportunity presented itself because later there might not be time. The biscuits were testimony to his wartime education.

Pouring himself another cup of coffee, the gambler sipped at it while he waited. He had drunk his way halfway to the bottom of the cup when Caitlyn returned.

"We buried Pa in his Sunday suit," she said as she placed a stack of clothes on the table. "But this was his go-to-town suit. And this was his hat. Most of the men coming to the auction today will be dressed like this. You'll look like one of them."

"I'd like to borrow a mule and a saddle, too," Chance said.

Caitlyn started to nod her okay, but abruptly replied, "I don't think that would be smart. Calloway knows we have two mules. If he checks and finds one gone, I don't think I could explain where it went."

The gambler agreed. It was a stupid risk, just to save his legs a few miles walk. He tucked the clothes under an arm and then took the shaving mug and razor from her hand. "Soon as I scrape away this stubble, I'll be going. I won't be back until the auction is just about to get under way."

As he turned to the back door, she reached out and grabbed his shoulder. He glanced back at her.

"Chance, be careful." She leaned to him, her lips meeting his.

"I'm always careful," he lied to her. "Today, I'll be doubly so."

Back in the barn, he used the water left from his bath for a shave. He then stripped away his own clothes, bundled and tied them in his shirt, and dressed in the borrowed clothing. The suit and shirt were simple black and white, but the black hat left him with arched eyebrows of doubt when he placed it atop his head. Farmer-style, the hat's crown was rounded without a hint of a tuck or crease. Likewise, the brim jutted straight out from the crown without the slightest bit of graceful curve. He was grateful for his lack of mirror: he was afraid that he looked his part too well!

Tossing his bundled clothing over a shoulder, he returned the mug and razor to the kitchen and then picked his way across the plowed fields to the woods surrounding the farm.

His own clothes hidden beneath a pile of dried leaves and branches, and the money tucked in a pocket of the borrowed coat, Chance located a thick clump of privet bushes and cherry laurels near the road leading to town and sat cross-legged on the ground behind them.

If he wished, he could reach out a hand and ease two privet branches aside to get a clear view of the Ragglin farm. However, the bushes were thick enough to hide him from view. That was the way he wanted it. Until a crowd gathered for the auction, he didn't intend to step from his hiding place. The less opportunity Calloway had of getting a look at him the better.

For two hours he did little except cross and uncross his legs while he watched the comings and goings of blue jays, red-winged blackbirds, and an occasional mockingbird as they flitted through the woods. Two plump squirrels that would have fit nicely in a stew pot scampered in the limbs overhead for about ten minutes, uncaring of the man beneath them, and never knowing the fate he had planned for them, if he had been carrying a hunting rifle.

Chance had just taken the first of the buttered, honeyed biscuits from the napkin when he heard the approach of horses and a wagon. He glanced up: the sun's position placed the hour near ten o'clock, two hours before the scheduled auction. He frowned as he edged away the privet branches and peered toward the farm.

A single buggy drawn by a matched team of black geldings trundled by on the road, heading straight for the Ragglin place, with three riders. The gambler recognized Brad Calloway immediately. To the blond weasel's left sat a man with a tin star on the breast of his black suit and the buggy's reins in his hand. Ben Daniel's sheriff, Chance supposed. Local authorities usually put in an appearance at public auctions. It provided the opportunity to shake a few hands, slap some backs, and kiss a couple of babies—all of which amounted to thickly spread manure to cultivate votes for the next election.

Chance could only guess at the third man's identity. But by the three-piece suit he wore, the gambler would have bet even money that this was the president of Ben Daniel's bank, who Caitlyn had mentioned accompanied Calloway on his first visit to the farm.

The gambler frowned as he watched the buggy pull up before the farmhouse and the three men step to the front porch. Until now Chance had never considered a local being in cahoots with Calloway. If either the sheriff or the banker were in league with Calloway, it could complicate matters.

Complicate them considerably, he thought as he released the branches when one of the sisters opened the house's door to the men. Chance shook away the dark possibility. If Calloway did have a local connection, it was too late to do anything about it, except play through the hand he held.

The first biscuit had disappeared, as well as the second and third, when the second horses came down the road. This time it was a wagon containing a farmer, his wife, and seven laughing children. Ten minutes later another wagon rolled onto the farm. After that wagons, buggies, and lone riders on horseback came in a steady stream.

The gambler watched them from his place behind the bushes while he ate his way through the three remaining biscuits, then wiped his mouth and dusted the crumbs from his borrowed suit with the napkin. The first few to arrive had swelled to a crowd of a hundred by eleven o'clock, and to two hundred thirty minutes later.

They turned the farm into a three-ringed circus as they wandered over every inch of the land. Chance watched each of the black-suited farmers walk to the fields, bend down, and scoop up a handful of dirt. This was carefully sifted through the fingers and usually sniffed. Twice the gambler saw men taste the soil as though their tongues could discern the minerals that composed it.

The second ring was the barn. The two mules were constantly paraded in and out of the structure to be inspected by each and every farmer, most running a hand over the animals' legs to check and double-check their soundness. And when they weren't feeling mules' legs and tugging up one animal's lips to check the teeth to determine the age of the stock, they were going over every inch of the various farm implements from the plow to the pitchforks. Chance could imagine the tally of value each man kept in his head as he went from harness to muck basket.

The final ring was the farmhouse itself. Although each

of the farmers took an obligatory tour of the home, the majority of their attention went to the fields and the barn. It was the wives and children who once inside the house never seemed to emerge. Here and there, the gambler did see a head, usually belonging to a child, poke from one of the windows and shout below or try to catch the head of one of the passersby below with a wet glob of spit.

Chance felt a twinge of guilt for requiring Caitlyn and her sisters to endure the probing and prying into the intimate nooks and crannies of their lives, which he was certain each of the women in the house was doing with a very critical eye. However, they would have to endure the intrusions if they wanted to keep their farm.

A pistol shot snapped the gambler's gaze to the farmhouse's front porch. There the sheriff stood, waving the would-be-buyers and parties who were simply interested in observing the spectacle of an auction to gather around him. Calloway emerged from the barn with his still-unidentified companion at his side.

Chance pushed to his feet and stretched. The waiting was over; noon had arrived. Stretching once again, he pushed from behind the bushes and walked to the crowd. When he reached the others, he hung back, remaining on the outer fringes.

The sheriff raised his pistol and fired another shot to silence the crowd. He then slipped a pocket watch from his coat and thumbed it open. "Folks, the official notice of this sale read that we would begin at straight-up noon, and that's what I intend to do."

He paused and let his gaze travel over the faces that were now turned to him. "Mr. Seese, here"—he waved an arm to Calloway—"has appointed me to serve as auctioneer for this sale. To make certain there ain't no complaints when we wind this up, I'm going to lay down a few rules here at the start. When someone bids, I want him to shout out plain and clear. Plus I want to see a hand raised or a name shouted with that bid so as I can see who's a-biddin'. That way there won't be no confusion. Understand?"

He waited again, until he received a murmur of approval from the crowd and a tilting of heads. He was a young man, yet to see his thirtieth year, Chance estimated. His accent said that he was a native son rather than a carpetbagger come south to gather what profit he could any way that he could.

"Mr. Seese and the president of our local bank have determined a beginning bid for this farm." The sheriff once more glanced at Calloway. "We'll start the bidding at that figure. Rule is that it will take at least ten dollars more to best another bid."

He waited again to make certain the crowd understood the bidding was to be in ten-dollar increments. When he was sure they had: "One more thing, if whoever wins the bid wants to auction off some of the items on the farm in a piecemeal fashion, he can do so after we've concluded our business here. Now, who'll open the bidding at a hundred dollars?"

Chance blinked at the low starting figure. While he did, twenty men raised their hands or called out their names. A two hundred bid from an individual brought two-fifty from another. The gambler kept silent as the bidding moved upward at fifty-dollar increments, then twenty-five, and finally by ten-dollar jumps.

"A flat fifteen hundred," shouted a man, who named himself Roy Comby.

No one else upped the bid.

"That's fifteen hundred from Mr. Roy Comby," the sheriff said after a moment's silence. "Fifteen hundred once, fifteen hundred . . ."

"Sixteen hundred," Chance bid, finally speaking, and raising an arm high to be identified. The hundred-dollar leap was intended to drive off further bids from Comby.

However, all it did was cause the man to crane his head around, seeking his bidding opponent, then shout, "Sixteen twenty-five."

"Seventeen hundred," Chance immediately answered.

"Seventeen fifty," came from Comby.

"Eighteen hundred."

Comby refused to back out. "Eighteen fifty."

Well aware of the limited funds in his pocket, the gambler once more upped the bid, "Two thousand."

A hushed whisper spread through the crowd as heads shifted from Chance to Comby. The farmer bit at his lower lip and started to speak, but a woman beside him jabbed his side with an elbow and shook her head. Comby glanced at the crowd.

"That's two thousand once," the sheriff called out while he scanned the faces of the crowd. "Two thousand twice—two thousand three times. Sold to the man standing at the back. Friend, step up here and pay Mr. Seese, and the title to this fine parcel of land will be signed over to you."

Chance waved an arm at the sheriff to acknowledge his words, then began to weave through the crowd that began to drift to their buggies and wagons. He felt Calloway's gaze on him even before he lifted his own eyes to the blond weasel. Ten feet from the farmhouse's front porch, he saw recognition spread over the man's face like a sickening wave of nausea. Calloway's eyes darted from side to side as though uncertain what he should do.

What he did was nothing. He stood there staring at the gambler as Chance climbed the steps to the porch, and shook the sheriff's extended hand. "Friend, I'll be glad to welcome you to our community as soon as you count out two thousand dollars and place it in Mr. Seese's hand there."

Chance pulled a wad of bills from his pocket, slowly counted the needed two thousand, and handed them to Calloway. "I sincerely hope that this is just the beginning of our business transactions, Mr. Seese." The tone of the gambler's voice left no doubt as to what other business he wished to conclude with Calloway.

The weasel swallowed hard when he accepted the money and dug into his coat for his wallet. The sheriff grinned and waved a hand to the banker. "This farm's yours lock, stock, and barrel as soon as Mr. Seese and you sign the title, Mr.—"

"Thief!"

That single word rasped from Calloway's throat as he opened his wallet to stuff the two thousand inside. The pieces of newspaper Chance had placed in the wallet were quite visible to both Calloway and the gambler. The blond weasel's head twisted to the sheriff, then Chance, and back to the sheriff.

"This man is a thief!" Calloway blurted. "His name is Brad Calloway—a blackhearted whoreson who attempted to rob me on my journey down the Mississippi!"

FIFTEEN

"Thief?" The word hissed between Chance's teeth.

"This blackguard is Brad Calloway!" The blond weasel pointed an accusing finger at the gambler. "I demand that he be arrested immediately!"

"You lying sonofabitch!" Chance's hands balled into fists with knuckles glowing a strained white. Calloway had gone too far. The robbery on the *Gulf Runner*, being thrown overboard, two weeks adrift on a ragged raft, all pressed down on the gambler, coiling his body like a fire-tempered, steel spring.

Chance's left shot out in a quick, straight jab that sank into Calloway's soft gut.

Air rushed from the weasel's lungs in a loud, surprised gust. His eyes bulged as though they were going to pop from their sockets. Calloway grasped his belly with both hands and doubled over.

Which was exactly what the gambler wanted. His right lashed out in an uppercut that ended against Calloway's left jaw. The man's head snapped back with his body following an instant later. He sprawled on the porch, groaning.

Half of Calloway's pain was an act. A fact that became all too clear to the gambler as he prepared to launch himself atop the murdering thief. Calloway's right hand went beneath his coat and came out with a cocked Army Colt. The pistol's muzzle swung upward to home on the gambler's chest.

There wasn't time to think; Chance reacted. He lunged to the left as Calloway's forefinger closed around the trigger. The thunder of exploding black powder roared in the gambler's ears. The buzz of hot lead scorched the air as the shot missed his side by a hairbreadth.

In the wake of that shot was a cloud of dark smoke that always accompanied the firing of black powder. Chance intended to use that blinding, acrid haze to his advantage. Before Calloway could trigger another round, he would be at his throat! He tensed, ready to—

Something hard and cold and unyielding slammed into the side of his head. Instead of billowing black smoke, streaking meteors raced before his eyes in a confused blur. The wooden porch that had been so solid beneath his feet but a heartbeat before was suddenly gone. He fell into the yawning chasm of darkness that opened under him.

Something cool and moist against his head brought the first crack of painful light in the sphere of blackness that enclosed the gambler. He tried to ignore it, because with the light came the throbbing inside his skull.

"Did you have to hit him so hard, Bill Hathaway?" A voice slipped through the widening crack; it was feminine and angry. "You might have killed him."

"Dammit, Caty, he attacked your uncle. What was I supposed to do?" The second voice was male and held more than a touch of pleading in its tone. " 'Sides, if I hadn't whopped him up side the head with the barrel of my Remington, your uncle was going to put a chunk of lead in him."

Chance tried to close off the voices, but they persisted, sending hairline fractures out from the crack in all directions. The blackness began to crumble.

"You didn't have to hit him so hard!" Chance recognized the voice now; it belonged to Caitlyn Ragglin.

"What does he mean to you anyway, Caty?" Chance still didn't know the male voice, although he was certain its owner was familiar with Caitlyn. He called her Katie, or was it Caty? Probably the latter, the gambler decided. He preferred Caitlyn. Caty was a name for a girl, and Caitlyn Ragglin was definitely *not* a girl!

"He's a friend who tried to help Lizzy, Marybeth, and me keep our land. Which is more than you did, Bill Hathaway, with your chest all puffed out and your voice a-booming as you auctioned off the farm," Caitlyn answered, her tone steeped in accusation.

In spite of the splitting pounding that resounded inside his skull, Chance pieced bits of the conversation together. The man Caitlyn spoke to was named Bill Hathaway. He had been the auctioneer—which meant he was the sheriff—who had coldcocked the gambler with a pistol before he could finish what he had started with Calloway.

"A friend? Dammit, Caty, this Calloway here is a thief! Didn't you hear your uncle? His name's Brad Calloway, and he is a thief." Hathaway made no attempt to disguise his irritation with the young woman.

"The name's Sharpe, Chance Sharpe." The gambler forced his eyes open. When the cottony haze dissipated, he saw that he lay atop a sofa in the Ragglins' parlor. Caitlyn knelt beside him, bathing the left side of his head with a cool cloth. The sheriff, Bill Hathaway, loomed above both of them. Chance repeated, "My name is Chance Sharpe. The man you know as John M. Seese is Brad Calloway. And he's more than just a thief. He's a murderer. He killed Caitlyn's uncle. I was the one who found the body."

Hathaway pulled a long-barreled Remington from a holster and aimed it at the gambler. "You can tell me your story once I get you locked up back in town." The sheriff tucked a hand behind his back and came up with a pair of handcuffs that he snapped securely around Chance's wrists. "If you're up to talking, you're feeling good enough to take a little ride with me. Get up from there real slow-like."

"Bill, didn't you hear him?" Caitlyn protested as Chance sat up and set off a double-time rhythm of pain in his head. "He's Chance Sharpe, and my uncle isn't my uncle, but Brad Calloway. It's Calloway you should be locking in jail."

"Up." Hathaway ignored her and motioned with a wave of the pistol for Chance to stand.

"Sheriff, you are making a mistake"—the gambler tried reason while he relearned the art of standing on two less-than-steady legs—"a big one. I'm not the man you want."

"Like I said, you'll get to say your piece once I've got you back in town." Again Hathaway motioned with the pistol's barrel. "Outside."

With a concerted effort to focus thought and muscle movement, Chance walked across the room to the open door that led to the porch. Gone was the three-ring circus that had played on the farm earlier. Gone too were Callo-way and the banker. The Ragglins' wagon and mules waited in front of the house.

"Climb up to the driver's seat, and don't try anything stupid," Hathaway ordered. "If I have to use this Reming-ton again, I'll be using the trigger and not the barrel."

Chance did as he was told, then lifted the reins when the sheriff took his place beside him. He clucked the mules forward at the lawman's command and headed the wagon toward Ben Daniel.

Caitlyn followed behind on foot, deriding the sheriff's intelligence, heritage, and ancestors in descriptive phrases that totally surprised the gambler. A mile from the farm, Hathaway ordered Chance to halt the mules and allowed Caitlyn to scramble into the back of the wagon. If he had thought offering the ride would silence her, he had mis-judged the situation. Even Chance's ears ached from her rantings by the time they had covered another of the seven miles to the town.

For the fourth time, Chance started with the poker game aboard the *Gulf Runner* and recounted every detail right down to the moment Hathaway's Remington slammed into the side of his head, robbing him of consciousness. The sheriff listened as he had done three times before; he nei-ther said a word nor offered a questioning expression. When the gambler concluded, he just sat there.

"Well?" Caitlyn finally demanded from where she sat in a chair beside Hathaway on the outside of the jail cell.

"Well, what?" The lawman looked at her as if he didn't know why she questioned him.

"What are you going to do about the *real* Brad Calloway, who murdered my *real* Uncle John?" she pressed.

Hathaway stood. "Right now, I intend to get myself some supper. It's getting late, and I haven't eaten since breakfast. If you'll promise to keep quiet, I might even consider buying you some dinner."

Chance eyed the lawman. It was hard not to see the admiration in his eyes when he looked at Caitlyn.

"Bill Hathaway, are you dumb as a post?" Caitlyn rolled her eyes in exasperation. "Haven't you heard one word Chance has said?"

"I heard every word he said," Hathaway answered sternly. "Heard it all four times that he said it. But that don't change a thing, Caty—"

Chance leaned his back against a wall of the cell and looked toward the ceiling. He knew what was coming next. He could better spend his time watching the few stars visible through the cell's only window.

"I still don't have a single shred of evidence to support one of his claims. However, John Seese has all those papers to prove that he *is* your uncle." Hathaway shook his head. "I don't understand what's got into you, Caty."

The sheriff shot Chance a suspicious glance, as though he knew what had been going on between the young woman and the gambler. It wasn't love or anything even like that the gambler saw in those dark eyes.

"If Chance *is* Calloway, then why didn't he just light out of town after he took the money? That would have been the easy thing to do. Instead he came back to the farm and tried to save it for us," Caitlyn demanded.

Hathaway stared at the young woman, then looked back at Chance. The sheriff's expression said that had he been in the gambler's shoes, he knew why he would have returned to the farm. That reason was called Caitlyn, or Caty in his case. His expression also held the hope that his reason wasn't Chance's reason. Finally, he said, "I admit that part throws me a bit. But it isn't hard evidence."

Caitlyn reached out and touched Hathaway's arm. "But it's the act of a man who is basically honest."

"If sneaking into a house and stealing a man blind can be called honest!" Hathaway answered with a snort.

"It was my money to begin with," Chance broke in. "It might have been sneaking, but it wasn't stealing. I don't believe there's a law on the books against sneaking."

The lawman shot the gambler a look that was meant to kill. Chance answered with a smile and a shrug.

Hathaway's head turned back to Caitlyn. "What do you want from me?"

"To listen to Chance and check out what he says," she replied. "That's not too hard, is it?"

Hathaway's gaze moved to the gambler. "If I were to be interested in verifying your identity, who would speak for you?"

"Would my attorney in New Orleans be sufficient?" Chance suggested.

"Wouldn't give two whoops and a holler for anything a lawyer said—nobody would around these parts, especially a New Orleans lawyer," the sheriff answered. "You'll have to do better than that."

"What about another officer of the law?"

Hathaway cocked an eyebrow with interest.

"Contact Detective Jean DeFoe of the New Orleans Police Department," Chance said. "He can identify me and vouch for me. I helped him with a murder case involving a family named Walsh last winter."

"Jean DeFoe," the lawman repeated, "detective with the New Orleans police?"

"Will he be good enough?" Chance asked with another smile, which only seemed to double Hathaway's irritation.

"Caty, if it'll make you happy, I'll wire this DeFoe come morning," the sheriff said when he turned back to the woman.

"I'd be happy if you sent the telegram tonight," she replied, emphasizing her words with a smile that was all sugar and molasses.

"Telegraph office is already closed for the night." Hathaway shook his head. "Morning will be soon enough."

Chance stepped to the bars at the front of the cell. "Calloway still has my money. He could vanish this night—him and his four friends."

"You're the sheriff," Caitlyn said. "You can get Willy to open the telegraph office and send the wire tonight."

Hathaway stared at her for a moment, then smiled. "I *am* the sheriff, aren't I? I guess it wouldn't hurt Willy none to open up and send that telegram."

"And I'd confiscate Calloway's money, if I were you," Chance suggested again. "He's walking on thin ice, and he knows it. With that bundle in his pocket, I wouldn't give even money on his still being in Ben Daniel come morning."

Hathaway eyed the gambler, but didn't reply. Instead, he said to Caitlyn, "I'm going to rouse Willy, care to go along for the walk?"

"I'd be delighted." The young woman slipped her arm through the arm Hathaway held out for her. As the sheriff opened the door to the jail, she glanced over a shoulder and smiled and winked at the gambler.

The door closed behind them, leaving Chance staring at the three empty cells across from his. He drew a deep breath, then stretched atop the cell's cot, trying not to dwell on his surroundings; it brought back too many memories of Andersonville and the cold sweat that always accompanied those memories.

You wanted to delay things, he told himself. *That's exactly what it looks like you've done.*

However, he had never considered having himself locked in jail to accomplish those ends. At least the three Ragglin sisters still possessed their land. And if Hathaway could convince the telegrapher of the importance of his wire, Jean DeFoe might have an answer here by tomorrow.

All of which did nothing to ensure that Calloway would be in Ben Daniel when the sun rose on a new day. Chance closed his eyes and sighed again. *And he still has my money in his pocket!* Maybe Caitlyn could convince Hathaway to confiscate the two thousand. She seemed quite capable of handling the lawman.

Nor did Hathaway seem to mind being handled by the young beauty. Chance smiled to himself. It would be something if Caitlyn and Hathaway were pricked by cupid's arrows amid all this—stranger things in this world had happened.

The piercing cry of a woman's scream shattered the gambler's thoughts. A deep rumble like the sound of a hundred men's voices came from outside. Chance pushed to his elbows, then stood atop the cot to reach the cell's window. Outside he saw nothing except the night. However, the voices were distinct now. They grew louder.

Another scream jerked the gambler's head around. The jail's door flew open and Caitlyn ran inside. Her face was as white as a bleached sheet when she darted to the cell. "Half the town is out there, and they want to hang you!"

SIXTEEN

Caitlyn's words rang in the gambler's head, echoing four times before he fully comprehended their meaning. And when he did, the best he could utter was "What?"

"We were about to walk into the cafe when the saloon doors swung wide and every man in Ben Daniel swarmed onto the street," she said. "They sounded like a pack of growling wolves—all wanting your blood. Calloway and his four friends were at the head of that pack, howling the loudest—"

Chance drew a steadying breath. Apparently he had overlooked one possible conclusion to this incident, but the blond weasel hadn't. He could well imagine the scenario. Calloway, with his gorillas, entered the saloon. For a man who had killed five men in one night aboard the *Gulf Runner,* involving a whole town in another murder would mean nothing. After a few drinks for the townsmen, probably purchased with the gambler's money, the five of them went to work suggesting that "real men" wouldn't leave matters to a court, but see to it that they were handled correctly— at the end of a rope. Fired by bottled courage, it wouldn't have taken long for those "men" to start calling each other "boys." Then there was no stopping them.

"Bill tried to reason with them," Caitlyn continued, "but all it got him was a fist in the face from one of Calloway's men. Three townsfolk then jumped him—"

Chance didn't need to hear anymore. With Hathaway out of the way, there was nothing between him and the mob that now stalked down Ben Daniel's main street. "Caitlyn, lock the front door, then try to find a key to this cell!"

141

While the gambler's fingers tried to squeeze through the cell's bars, Caitlyn pivoted and snapped the lock to the jail's door. She then turned to Hathaway's desk, yanking drawers out and throwing papers into the air as she searched for the key.

"If you stumble on a spare pistol in there, bring it too," the gambler said.

"Here's the key!" Caitlyn held it up, then shook her head. "But I can't find a gun."

"The key is enough." Chance waved her to him.

She slipped the key into the lock, and swung the door open. Chance stepped out, grasped her shoulders, and pushed her inside. He had locked the cell door before she could blink her confusion. "It's not a nice place to be, but you'll be safe here."

"Chance, let me out of here. You'll need . . ." Her words were drowned beneath the splintering of wood.

The gambler spun around to see the door fly from its hinges. The two men who had thrown their weight against the locked obstacle hit the floor, rolling.

Had those two been all, Chance wouldn't have worried. However, a tidal wave of angry, shouting men flooded into the jail. Chance's head snapped around, searching for a back door to the jail—there was none! In a wide stance, he stood his ground and waited.

The first man to reach him went down when the gambler threw a right squarely into his nose. The second fell from an equally well placed left. Then there was no hope. They swarmed over him, pinning his arms and legs, dragging him outside into the night.

"Take him to the old oak out at the edge of town!" a faceless voice shouted and was answered by a chorus of cheers.

Once again the mob surged forward with Chance riding its crest. The gambler's eyes darted from side to side, seeking some means of escape. All he saw was Bill Hathaway being held by four men to one side of the street. The sheriff's face was dark and wet with blood that dripped from a cut on his forehead. For a moment he stared at

Chance, then his eyes rolled downward as though in shame at being unable to contain the lynch mob.

"You gonna dance real pretty on the end of a rope, Calloway." A man to the gambler's right leered, then spat into Chance's face. "You gonna pay for trying to cheat them Ragglin girls out of their farm."

Several men around the gambler laughed as he was dragged farther down the street.

"Dead man!" When Chance first heard the shouted words, he thought they were describing him. But the cry rang out again, "Dead man!"

The angry shouts of the mob behind the gambler grew to a murmur of uncertainty.

"We got a dead man here," the voice shouted again. "He was found on the river."

"We have another dead man here." Chance recognized this voice as belonging to Brad Calloway. "Soon as we hang him from the old oak at the end of town."

There were several men who raised their voices in approval, but the majority of the mob remained silent.

"Think you boys might want to take a look at this man 'fore you go hangin' the wrong man."

The men holding Chance jerked him around. The mob opened wide to reveal four men carrying a corpse by his arms and legs. A smell of decay was carried on the night breeze. They placed the dead man on the ground, holding a burning torch above the body. The gambler swallowed. The last time he had seen John M. Seese, the dead man had been in better condition. But there was no doubt as to the corpse's identity.

One of the men who had carried the body turned and waved a hand to a boy who had followed them. George Peters, or whatever his name was, stepped forward. Behind came Sam Clemens and Odell. Chance grinned, never happier to see three people before in his life.

"These men and this boy found this body in a skiff upstream. I think the sheriff ought to take a look at him. They claim the man's name is John Seese," the townsman said.

To the side Chance saw Hathaway shake off the men holding him, push through the mob, and approach the corpse.

"He's carrying a wallet, sir," George spoke up. "There's letters in it addressed to a John Seese. There's also fifty dollars in there."

Hathaway glanced at Chance, then knelt beside the corpse to pull the wallet from the dead man's coat. It took only seconds for him to extract the letters and read the name John M. Seese. "It appears that all of us may have made a mistake."

"Sonofabitch!" The curse was growled, rather than spoken. The source was one of Calloway's gorillas, who broke from the crowd and started to run for a hitching rail lined with horses.

He made it two strides before five of Ben Daniel's townsmen jumped him, bringing him to the ground. Then all hell broke loose!

A second of Calloway's goons, apparently recognizing the tables had abruptly turned, pulled a pistol and shot two men in the stomach as he tried for the horses and escape. His life ended in the blast of a shotgun—both barrels at once. What was left of the man was thrown ten feet in the air before it hit the ground.

The hands and arms that pinned Chance were suddenly gone as Ben Daniel's law-abiding citizenry forgot about the man they were determined to hang minutes ago and turned their wrath on Calloway's two remaining henchmen. Fists and lead flew, but the gambler couldn't see the results of either as the mob closed and surged forward.

However, he was certain that Calloway was not a target for the shouting men. He scanned the crowd, searching for the weasel's telltale blond mane. He didn't see it.

The hollow pounding of horse's hooves spun Chance around. He found the blond man—Calloway, thrown low to a bay's neck, had found a mount and now spurred it from the town.

Since arriving in Ben Daniel, the gambler had postponed confronting the murderer. Unless he moved quickly there might not be time to repay the blond weasel for all the kindness he had shown him.

Chance darted to the hitching rail and untied a buckskin that stood at the head of the horses there. Looping the reins over the animal's head, he swung into the saddle, pulled the horse's head around, and slammed booted heels into the mount's flanks.

Calloway's bay held a quarter of a mile lead on the buckskin as Chance raced westward past the last building in Ben Daniel. Again the gambler dug his heels into his mount's sides, urging it to greater speed. It didn't help; Calloway used the ends of his reins like a whip, slapping them from one side of the bay to the other.

It wasn't speed, however, but endurance that began to tell after the horses' hooves burned up two miles. The buckskin slowly began to gain on the bay. A fact that apparently caught Calloway's attention. He swung around in the saddle, lifted his Colt, and fired.

The shot went high and wide, but drove home the point that the blond weasel was armed, while the only weapon Chance carried was the stiletto sheathed inside his right boot. Although the double-edged blade had proved its value on more than one occasion, it was of little use against a six-shooter.

Blue and yellow flame belched from the Colt's muzzle a second time, as Calloway reined the bay from the road into a stand of pines to the left. Chance's legs rose and fell as he spurred the buckskin after the man.

Throwing himself against the horse's neck, the gambler ducked beneath the low-slung branches that sought to drag him from his mount's back. When the buckskin bolted out from the trees, Chance sat straight in the saddle. A frown creased his brow.

The bay ran across an open meadow—riderless!

Wha . . . ?

His half-thought question was answered by the resounding blast of a Colt from behind him. Hot lead, buzzing like an angry hornet, sliced the air just above the gambler's right shoulder. Chance once again threw himself forward onto the buckskin's neck and spurred the horse forward. Another shot rang out behind him.

Four, the gambler thought, mentally keeping count of the fired rounds.

Swinging the buckskin to the right, he rode across the open field, then snatched the animal around and spurred him toward the opposite side. He didn't like setting himself and the animal up as Calloway's moving targets, but until the sixth load in the Colt's chamber was spent, he had no other choice. All his life he had played the odds. This was no different; he bet that he was far enough from the murderer that the Colt would prove inaccurate.

A fifth blue and yellow blossom of exploding black powder shot from the pines. A humorless smile moved across the gambler's lips as the fifth shot cut through the night behind him. Not only had Calloway wasted another round, but the flame from the muzzle had given away his position. The weasel stood between the fork of a twin-trunked pine.

Abruptly Chance wrenched the buckskin around and reversed the direction of his ride again. The maneuver worked. Calloway fired his sixth shot, which hit harmlessly into the ground ten feet short of its intended target.

When the gambler tugged the buckskin's head around again, it was to rein the horse directly toward the double-trunked pine. Surprisingly, Calloway stood his ground, vainly attempting to reload the old Army Colt until Chance was only twenty feet away. Then he tossed the spent weapon aside and ran.

It was too late. Chance edged around the pine and leaped from the saddle. Full weight, he slammed into Calloway's back, sending both of them tumbling to the wood's bed of brown needles.

The gambler gained his feet an instant before the blond weasel. That instant was all he needed to greet the rising man with a right to his left jaw. The blow threw Calloway to his back.

The man shook his head and pushed upward. His face

met the toe of the gambler's boot, and he went sailing back to the needles. Blood oozed from one of the nostrils of his nose when he glanced up and hissed, "You bastard."

The profanity brought him another right to the jaw. Then Chance was atop him, both fists pounding his face without mercy. The gambler felt bone crush beneath his blows. Chance didn't stop. Again and again the gambler's fists rose and fell.

"Sharpe!" a voice barked in the night. "That's enough! Stop or you'll kill him. I want enough left of that son-ofabitch to hang."

Chest heaving, Chance caught himself. He looked up, balled fists dropping limply to his side. Bill Hathaway sat astride a horse ten feet to the right.

"Let him be, Sharpe," the sheriff said. "He ain't going nowhere, except to my jail. Get off of him, I've got him now."

Begrudgingly, the gambler pushed to his feet and stared down at the unconscious man beneath. Blood oozed from a dozen opened cuts on that face. The lawman was right; Calloway wasn't going anywhere.

"You'd better pick up that buckskin you borrowed," Hathaway said as he stepped from the saddle and walked to Calloway. "I'd hate to have to hang you for a horse thief. I personally know the buckskin's owner, and he don't take to anyone riding him except himself."

Chance glanced around, unable to find a trace of the animal. "Maybe you can put a good word in for me with the owner."

"I doubt it." Hathaway shook his head while he snapped handcuffs around Calloway's wrists. "I own that horse."

Chance groaned aloud, as he turned and started to search for the missing buckskin.

SEVENTEEN

The riverboat's steam whistle set Chance's temples to pounding as he stepped onto Ben Daniel's main street dressed in new hat, shirt, and suit. He also wore a new watch fob with derringer attached and a holstered .44 Colt behind his coat. He would have the barrel sawed off to his preference for a belly-gun once he reached New Orleans.

If I reach New Orleans, he thought as the paddle-wheeler's whistle pierced the air once again. His gaze moved to the end of the street where Ben Daniel's wooden pier pushed out into the Mississippi. A white-painted sternwheeler bearing the name *Colonel Bullfinch* leisurely made a 180 degree turn and steamed portside toward the wharf.

The gambler muttered a curse as he started toward the town's cafe. Although Philip Duwayne had wired the requested five hundred promptly, the Arkansas legal system still shuffled along. Two days after Brad Calloway's scam had crumbled, Sheriff Bill Hathaway still had not cleared Chance in the John M. Seese murder. The lawman *did* assure him that no formal charges would be brought. However, he also added a policeman's favorite qualification—"Don't leave town." Not until everything was wrapped up. Nor would Hathaway even estimate when that wrap-up would be completed.

Which meant the gambler's "great adventure" was still continuing, while those he had shared it with would see theirs an hour from now when they stepped onto the decks of the *Colonel Bullfinch* and pulled away from Ben

Daniel. And Chance had ensured that would be the case; in a pocket to his new coat were three steamer tickets for Clemens, Odell, and George who-claimed-his-last-name-to-be-Fink-again.

It was these that he handed his friends when he entered the cafe and walked to where they sat with Caitlyn and her sisters. Clemens and Odell eyed the gambler as though uncertain of what to say and were silenced before they spoke by a shake of Chance's head. However, George beamed, excused himself, and while clutching his ticket ran from the cafe to "reconnoiter" the vessel that would take him the rest of the way downriver. Chance took the boy's vacated seat and ordered a cup of coffee from the waitress.

"Mr. Twain here was telling us everything that happened after they discovered that you were missing," Caitlyn said.

Chance lifted an eyebrow and looked at his friend. "I'd be interested in hearing that myself, Mr. Twain, or do you still answer to 'king'?"

Clemens grinned, ignored the last comment, and began, "It's like I was telling these lovely young ladies. When we discovered the skiff with the deceased Mr. Seese lying in its bottom, we put two and two together and came up with the fact that you had somehow managed to fall into the floodwaters and get yourself drowned."

"That was after we searched every inch of that island for you, Mr. Chance," Odell amended Clemens's version. "That took all of one day and half the next. Even then, we weren't none too sure what had happened, though we was pretty sure that you had up and drowned yourself."

Clemens cleared his throat. "Be that as it may, we searched Seese's body and discovered the letters and money. We were honor-bound to find a representative of the law and turn the body in."

"It weren't nigh that simple," Odell broke in again. "We spent another half day tryin' to figure out whether or not to keep the fifty and cut the skiff and the dead man loose. Mr. Clem—Twain did finally convince George and me it would be safer if we turned the body over to the law. He said there might be some reward in it for us."

Chance grinned while Clemens gave an embarrassed shrug. That embarrassment lasted for the blink of an eye, then he was back to his tale:

"We left the island with the skiff tied to the raft. When we reached Ben Daniel, we learned that Chance here had been arrested for murdering your uncle. We also saw Brad Calloway and knew something was terribly amiss. That's when we called to those townsfolk and showed the body. It was our quick thinking that saved Chance here from wearing that rope necktie."

Chance glanced at Odell, who only rolled his eyes and sighed at the writer's exaggeration. The gambler let his friend's remarks slide by without comment. There was no need jabbing pins in his story again.

"Mr. Twain, you should set everything that happened to you and Chance down in writing." Marybeth beamed with obvious admiration for the writer.

"Oh, yes!" Lizzy said, her face also glowing with enthusiasm. "This would make such a better story than those about frogs and such-like in your first book."

"My first book?" Clemens's eyebrows arched high in interest. "You ladies are familiar with my first literary effort?"

Before the sisters could answer, Chance turned to his friend. "You and Odell should be heading down to the pier. Literary efforts don't mean a hill of beans to a riverboat captain. If you two aren't on deck when he decides to pull out, it'll make no nevermind to him."

A flicker of disappointment raced across Clemens's face for a moment, then vanished. He nodded, pushed from the table, and held a hand out to Chance. "My friend, I wish you were going with us, and I want to thank you for the small loan and ticket. I'll see that you're repaid as soon as I reach New Orleans and wire my bank in New York."

The gambler stood and accepted the proffered hand.

"I'd like to think that you would have done the same for me."

"I'd like to think that, too." Clemens winked at the gambler, then bowed to the Ragglin sisters, and left with Odell following behind him.

"I think that I'll go see the riverboat off," Lizzy said, and was echoed by Marybeth: "Me too."

Which left Chance and Caitlyn alone at the table. The young woman smiled as she watched her sisters run after the writer, who escorted the two lovelies toward the pier—one on each arm. "They're quite taken by your friend, Mr. Twain."

Her brown eyes shifted to the gambler. He thought he detected a hint of sadness veiled in their diamond sparkle. "You should be aboard that riverboat."

Chance shrugged. "Not according to your friend Bill Hathaway. He wants me to stick around Ben Daniel for a while."

"He's only doing his job." She made no attempt to disguise the defensive edge to her voice.

The gambler smiled and reached out to take her hand. "He's a good man, Caitlyn. Although I think that he'd make a better farmer than a lawman."

She returned his smile with a slight blush to her cheeks. "I was thinking along the same lines myself."

Giving her hand a squeeze, he said, "Why don't we walk down to the pier and see the others off?"

With a nod, she rose. Before they could step from the table, Bill Hathaway entered the cafe and walked to them. "Caty, I'd like a few moments alone with Chance, if you don't mind?"

Doubt shadowed her face as she glanced at the gambler, but she left without comment.

"Religion's a strange thing." The sheriff settled to a chair and motioned Chance back to his. "Have you ever noticed that?"

The gambler frowned at Hathaway. "Bible thumping isn't what's on your mind."

"No, but it was on Johnny Haynes's mind before he died."

Chance's eyes narrowed. Haynes was one of Calloway's gorillas. He had been shot in the chest the night Ben Daniel had decided to fit the gambler for a rope necktie. The local doctor hadn't given the man better than fifty-fifty chance of recovering from the wound. "Haynes died?"

"About an hour ago," the lawman said with a nod. "But not before he asked to see a preacher. Seems his ma raised him according to the good book, and he wanted to own up to his wrong doings before he had to look Saint Peter in the eye."

"And?" Chance pressed.

"And he confessed everything—in writing with his signature neat and tidy after the final line. The preacher witnessed the confession, making it all legal-like." Hathaway eased his hat to the back of his head.

"What do you mean by 'everything'?"

"Scuttling the *Gulf Runner* and murdering John Seese," the sheriff replied. "And a hell of a lot more. Enough to ensure Calloway and the other two an appointment with a hangman."

Hathaway reached into a pocket to withdraw a roll of bills that he tossed to the gambler. "Looks like this belongs to you after all. Nineteen hundred total—Calloway was buying the rounds the night the boys decided to see how you'd look dancing from a rope."

Chance did a quick count to confirm the tally. Nineteen hundred remained of the original bankroll Calloway had taken from him. Considering the circumstances, it was more than the gambler had hoped to ever recover.

"Maybe you should use some of that to buy you a ticket on that riverboat waiting down at the pier," Hathaway suggested.

Chance glanced up. "You mean, I'm free to leave?"

Hathaway tilted his head. "If I need you for the trial, I know how to get in touch with you. That Detective DeFoe offered to give me any assistance I needed—'specially if it had anything to do with locking you away for the rest of your natural days."

Chance pushed from the table and tipped his hat to the sheriff. "I won't say that it's been a pleasure, because it hasn't."

As the gambler started to turn, Hathaway called to him. "One more thing, Sharpe. I'd just as well never see you in this town again. We ain't got much need of gamblers in Ben Daniel. 'Specially gamblers who go around stealing horses. Fact is, the owner of a certain buckskin has indicated that he intends to press charges if you aren't on that riverboat when it pulls away."

"That's not very neighborly, Sheriff." Chance turned and faced the lawman.

"Sharpe, I don't know what happened between you and Caty while you were out at the farm. Truth is I don't want to ever know," Hathaway said. "But as far as Caty is concerned—any more neighborlying with her, I'll be the man doing it. Do I make myself clear?"

"Perfectly." Chance smiled. "And, Sheriff, you'd be a crazy man if you didn't consider turning that pistol you're toting into a plowshare."

Leaving Hathaway with a confused expression plastered on his face, the gambler pivoted and left the cafe. There was a paddlewheeler waiting for him.

"He ain't nowhere to be found 'board this boat." Odell stared at his two companions and shook his head. "Ain't nobody seen him come 'board."

Clemens struck a match and lit the cigar clamped between his teeth. "If I were a wagering man, I'd bet that a certain ticket aboard this fine vessel was exchanged for hard cash shortly after George ran from the cafe."

Chance was a gambling man, but he wouldn't have taken that bet even with fifty-to-one odds.

"It's a great adventure he's living," Clemens continued. "And George isn't one to throw something like that away."

Chance lit his own cigar, turned, and leaned against the boiler deck rail. "I'll be damned."

"Without a doubt." Clemens turned his gaze, following the direction of the gambler's stare.

There on the Arkansas side of the river, near the bank, rode a raft that had once been part of a larger logger's raft. At the rudder to that rudimentary sailing vessel stood a boy with bright red hair. He lifted an arm high and waved as the sternwheeler churned its way past him.

"A great adventure," Clemens murmured more to himself than to his two companions, who returned the boy's wave.